SISSIES IN HEAT

5-Book Erotica Bundle

Femdom Feminization, Sissification, Crossdressing

RAE ROBINSON

CONTENTS

THE COUGAR'S SHY SISSY

MY WIFE'S NEW LOVER

BLIND DATE

FEMDOM MAID

BROKEN BY MY BULLY

SISSIES IN HEAT
THE COUGAR'S SHY SISSY

THE COUGAR'S SHY SISSY

CHAPTER 1

JULIA GLENDOWER STEPPED into the restaurant looking like a star. I definitely had stars in my eyes.

Well. She *was* a star.

A retired actress, to be more specific. Not the Hollywood kind, though that didn't really matter to me. She'd starred in several small-screen productions as *Juliana* Glendower and had been a force in the national theater scene in the 1980s, even releasing a dance album with a track that became a Top Fifty hit in 1985. Now she was nearing sixty and for the first time in a decade had moved back to her hometown. For what? No one knew exactly, but I guess it was to do the things retired people were supposed to do.

I cleared my throat and stood up as she approached me.

"I almost couldn't recognize you in that suit, Jasper," she said, giving me an air kiss on the cheek.

"Thank you, Mrs. Glendower," I said, blushing. I was wearing an old hand-me-down jacket that belonged to my mom's boyfriend. It was a little big on me, and the pants just about swept the floor when I walked, but I'd wanted to look extra professional for tonight. "And thank you for the opportunity, once again."

She smiled and slipped into the other end of the curved leather seat. She fished a small gold mirror from her handbag and began fixing her hair and lipstick, ignoring the patrons that were staring at her. They had to know who she was.

I took my time enjoying her look too. She had long blonde hair that shone like silk and thick, juicy lips that could make any man think some very dirty thoughts. Her top-heavy frame made the wrap dress she was wearing bulge out in all the right ways, and as she deftly moved her fingers to dab onto the fresh coating of her lipstick, her breasts shifted and rubbed against each other in a not-so-subtle way. She was definitely wearing a bra because I could see the outline of the straps on her shoulders, but it wasn't giving her too much support. Though I kind of liked that. It made her breasts seem all the more real.

Did she *know* how good-looking she was? Even in her sixties?

"Did you practice your lines?" she asked once she was done with her touch-up.

"I did, Mrs. Glendower," I answered.

She glanced down at her watch. "Good. Terry's still on his way, so we can go over your lines until then."

A waiter interrupted us then with the menus. I watched her closely as she perused the menu, looking over the selection of wine and appetizers. She ordered a vodka martini. The waiter broke into a smile and started excitedly talking to her about one of her TV movies.

What the fuck am I doing in a fancy-ass restaurant with this exquisite actress right across from me? I wondered as I listened to their back and forth.

I was a twenty-five-year-old college dropout who still lived with his mom. I didn't really have any aspirations. I spent my days killing time on the internet and working my shifts at my fancy-schmancy job sorting produce at a grocery store. When Julia moved to the large bungalow-style house across the street from us—the one that had been built by some bored and impulsive architect and had been left vacant since I was a teen because no one in our town had that kind of money—I didn't even know who she was until Mom filled me in. I was pretty good at spying on her from that point on, mostly because circumstances made it so that it would've been impossible *not* to, since my bedroom window perfectly lined up to her own.

Julia didn't know this, but I'd once seen her braless.

Just one time. It was pretty neat. Her tits were full and heavy and tear-drop-shaped and looked like they were DDs. Her nipples were swollen and as big as teats like they'd been sucked on by many lucky men over the years.

Now, those DDs were just a few feet away from me.

I mean, I would've been very happy just to keep spying on her. But everything changed the day she saw me washing my mom's car.

Julia was out on her front porch wearing a sundress and reading a book. She had a smart-looking corgi decked out next to her, catching the morning sunlight and beaming at everyone just the way corgis do. Of course I'd been checking her out from the corner of my eye while I was tending to the car, but when she

4

caught me looking at her she set down her book and called me over.

"Do you know who I am?" she asked.

"Yes, ma'am," I said.

"Hm," she said. "And you are?"

"I'm Jasper, ma'am," I said. "Jasper Miller."

A bead of sweat trickled down my forehead, and I nervously brushed it away. I didn't have much experience talking to the other sex, let alone a gorgeous cougar.

She asked me a few more questions, and I had to tell her with a straight face that I was a college drop-out living with my mom and her boyfriend.

She looked at me thoughtfully while her corgi sniffed at my boots.

"Have you ever wanted to get into acting?" she asked.

"*Acting?*"

The question threw me off guard at first. Like I said, I'd never really had anything in my life I was truly passionate about, let alone dreams of becoming famous. I'd trudged through life so far without a lot of luck by my side and my mom kept rubbing in my face that I had no career and I was destined to live with her forever. She was right. My friends all had great jobs and pretty girlfriends...while I was broke and had no one. Time was slipping like sand through my fingers and I was drifting further and further away from who a twenty-five-year-old guy was supposed to be.

"Look up at my eyes, boy," Julia said suddenly. "And answer the question."

My eyes snapped up and heat pooled into both my cheeks. I

didn't even know I'd been absent-mindedly staring at her breasts.

"Yes, ma'am," I lied. "I've thought about acting. Since I was a baby. My mom put me in a couple of baby commercials by the time I was teething."

She arched a perfectly lined eyebrow up at me. She seemed surprised at what I'd just said—none of which was true, of course.

"You should know I work as a scout. Did you know that, Jasper?" she said.

I shook my head, not quite sure what she was getting at.

She gave me an infectious smile. "I'm actually seeing a producer for dinner tomorrow and I'd like you to come along," she said. "Though you'll have to wear something better than that grimy shirt and those dirty boots."

She told me to wait on the porch and she went inside her house. Several minutes later, she came out and handed me a folder. My heart pounded as I opened up the folder. It contained a short script, printed neatly in that standard screenwriting font. Julia told me to memorize them and come to the restaurant at seven.

"You're lucky she's giving you the opportunity," my mom said when I hurried back to the house and told her the news. She took a drag from her cigarette and tossed her head at me. "Don't fuck this one up."

I wasn't planning to fuck it up, though I still wasn't sure exactly what someone like Julia had seen in me.

Now, with her sitting right there in front of me, still patiently talking to the nosy waiter, I couldn't believe she was giving me a lifeline. I had it all planned out in my mind. I was going to bag this audition and I was going to be a rising star, and I'd impress all the execs so much that they'd send me off to Hollywood. Julia Glendower would be my secret lover, and my mom would be one proud mom.

Once the waiter left, Julia went over my lines with me.

"How could you do this to me, Sienna?" I spoke in a hushed voice because I was *really* self-conscious. "How dare you, uh, cheat on me?"

"Because cheating was the only way I could bring the passion out of you," Julia said, her lashes flashing at me through her sizzling gaze.

As we did the scene snippet over and over again, I got lost in time. Julia had a way of making you feel emotions you never knew you were capable of feeling. I felt angst, longing, and the ache of having a girlfriend betray you even though I'd been single my whole life. I felt like I was sucked into a universe where we were no longer even acting and I was *normal.*

Her pull was so powerful it took me a while to realize that she was slipping closer and closer to me through the curved seat.

Our arms finally touched.

My breath hitched.

She took my hand and placed it on her lap. Her hand was full of soft lines and I wanted to curl my fingers around hers and feel her gentle, feminine warmth.

"Uh?" Was this part of the scene? I was so lost I didn't even know what to say.

I didn't recall a seduction scene in the script she'd given me…

Julia looked so calm, though. So calm even as she was steadily pushing my hand lower down her dress.

I gulped and quickly whipped my head around to check if anyone had caught the move. Surprisingly, everyone seemed to be enjoying their meals, and no one was giving me the stink-eye. I tried to catch Julia's gaze but she didn't even look at me. With her poker face on, she was just casually inspecting her drink. Then she took a long sip.

Is this really happening?

When my fingers grazed her bare skin, I almost squealed. She wasn't wearing any pantyhose. Didn't women her age wear pantyhose? She was a *cougar,* alright. The skin of her thigh was so soft. Like…butter. Whipped butter. I'd never touched a woman like this.

Every touch was like a lightning strike to my chest.

I watched as Julia smiled at no one in particular as she finally thrust my hand between her legs.

CHAPTER 2

FUCK ME. SHE isn't wearing panties!

My fingers combed through her lower lips. She had a little peach fuzz going on and it was very nice to the touch. A horny cougar's pussy. There was so much to explore.

Julia let go of my hand and cupped the stem of her martini glass. Her thighs parted until her knee rested on my dress pants. *She wants more.* Taking a deep breath, I gently preened her pussy lips apart and slithered my fingers into what lay beneath. Folds upon folds, and nestled at the top was the wet, ripe nub of her clit. I started massaging there with my middle finger, hoping I had on a poker face that was half as good as hers.

Between my own legs, I had what was probably the biggest erection of my life.

The diners to the left of us dropped a fork to the ground with a clatter. The woman, who looked about in her 30s, dipped down to search for it. When she didn't rise back up, I knew she could probably see the surprise party going on underneath our tablecloth.

Reluctantly, I took my hand out of Julia's pussy lips.

The woman shot me a dirty look and muttered something to her husband.

"Don't be shy," Julia whispered. Her voice was soft yet stern at the same time. She still didn't look at me. She was glaring at the woman, as if daring her to say something.

Did she like this? The thrill of doing it in public?

Possibly getting me in trouble?

Shivering, I plunged my fingers back in again. I traced her linings from top to bottom before paying attention to her nub once more. She was getting *really* wet. I could feel her body temperature rising, her pleasure swelling, and all my thoughts slowed down, becoming sludge in my head.

Julia clamped her thighs around my fingers, enclosing them in her wetness. She pressed herself against me and almost instantly my fingertips were soaked. She brought her glass to her lips and kissed the rim, wiping her fresh lipstick on there to leave a kiss print.

God, what I would do to have those lips on mine!

I pleasured her with my fingers, picking up speed. I wanted to make her cum more than anything, but the truth was I had no idea what I was doing. I was just copying stuff I'd seen in porn. But could she tell? I suddenly felt completely inadequate. How could I have even thought that I could make an accomplished actress cum? I was a nobody.

To my shock, my cock hardened. I wasn't sure why. I was ready to blow my load at the thought of disappointing Julia...how fucked up was that? *Why?* I could just imagine her being pissed off at me, and she'd vow never to talk to me again.

No. I couldn't let that happen.

"Get down there," she said.

I froze. *Wait.* She wanted me to get down under the table? That could only mean one thing.

My stiff cock groaned with longing.

I quickly snuck a glance at our surroundings, and once I decided the coast was clear, I wriggled myself through the space between the table and our leather seat.

In the darkness, I stuck my tongue out and began tasting Julia's cunt. I felt her buckle and she pressed her thighs around my head like she wanted to squish my neck, resting her feet on my back. I used my hand to pry her lips open and nibbled at her clitoris before sucking on it gently like it was a nipple. If someone were to drop something again they'd catch me for sure, and how fucking dirty would they think I was to have my tongue all over the private parts of a woman who was thirty years my senior? The thought excited me a little too much…

Here it was, my first sexual experience with a woman and I was loving it. There was something so primal about her mature scent, making both my mind and my body move to please.

She was a Goddess…

In a bold move, I dragged Julia's hips further down and propped her butt slightly up so I could get access to her tempting cougar butthole. Her smell and taste down there quickly began overpowering me. I stuck my tongue inside her hole and felt her clench, a sexy moan escaping her lips. The Goddess was on the cusp of an orgasm.

Any minute now…

"Julia!" a man boomed from behind me. "Looking as lovely as

always!"

I gasped and almost knocked my head on the underside of the table. Julia gave me a kick to push me away. Then her legs were gone. I could hear what sounded like air kisses being exchanged, and then her legs reappeared.

"It looks like our young man is a little late," she said. "Disappointing."

"Are you sure about him then?"

There was a pause. "That remains to be seen. Obviously."

"You should school him about first impressions," he said, chuckling.

Sweating, I pulled my knees up to my chest and crouched toward the middle of the table so I wouldn't accidentally get kicked by Julia's conversing friend. The taste of her pussy and ass was still on my lips.

Crap. What the fuck do I do?

Someone came to the table, their dress shoes tip-tapping on the tiled floor. A waiter. "Could I get you anything from the bar, sir?"

"Bring me a double scotch, please. On the rocks." There was a pause. "Would you direct me to the restroom?"

"Certainly, sir," the waiter said. "Please follow me."

I waited until their legs disappeared and then I scrambled out, giving Julia a sheepish grin while brushing away the web of dust that had stuck to my suit.

She smiled back at me like she didn't almost just get me in trouble. Like I hadn't—just seconds earlier—furiously eaten her booty.

She likes putting me in danger, I thought.

We sat in awkward silence until the man—he had to be Terry—returned. He was about as well-dressed as I'd expected and he towered over me as I shook his hand.

"So this is Jasper," he said, giving me the once-over.

"Pleased to meet you, mister...uh...mister..."

"Mr. Burke," he said. His voice seemed to rumble from his chest as he spoke. "So I'm assuming Jules told you about me. I'm a filmmaker and producer, and I've personally worked with her on about a dozen productions. What makes you think you can work alongside an icon like Jules?"

Julia cast me a curious look.

"I'm not sure I can, but I'd like to give it my best shot, Mr. Burke, and I've watched all her movies," I said. "You could say I'm a huge fan."

The lie had vomited out of me faster than I could stop myself.

"Oh? What would you say is your favorite?" he asked.

"Uh...*Felicity's Fate*, Mr. Burke," I blubbered. I only knew that one because mom wouldn't stop shutting up about it. "I've watched it since I was a baby."

That seemed to impress him. The waiter came by again and we ordered off the menu. To play it safe, I ordered the same thing Julia wanted: creamed lobster with a side of asparagus and potatoes. By the time the food came, I couldn't help but feel like a fish out of water. Julia and Terry were so good-looking and exuded status and all this greatness and then there was just...me.

"He has soft features," Mr. Burke said out of the blue.

Soft features? What did he mean by that?

"He does," Julia said. "I'm sure he'll look even smaller on the screen. Don't you?"

"I believe so," he said.

They were both talking like I wasn't even there.

"But why don't we test it out?" Mr. Burke added. "I've got the goods right here." He patted something to his right then produced a leather tote, which he handed to me.

Julia clapped her hands, and her tits clapped right along too. "Great," she said, then she turned to me. "We'd like you to change into the dress and heels we've got in there. We really need to get an idea on how we can market your look."

I blinked. "A dress? Heels?" I asked. "Like…girl's clothes?"

"That's right, Jasper," Julia said. She was keeping her face very still. "It's part of our audition tonight." She flipped toward me, resting her eyes on mine. Those steamy, hypnotizing blue eyes. "Look, I'll be blunt. You don't have to do it just because we say so. But if you're truly interested in this role, I'd suggest you think before you act. I don't want just anybody. I want someone who's truly committed and isn't afraid to show it."

"The restrooms are right at the end of the corridor there," Mr. Burke said helpfully, pointing to the end of the dining hall.

I swallowed. My throat was suddenly as dry as dust. I mean, it was definitely a weird request. If they wanted me to play a *woman*, I most definitely wasn't going to agree to it. I was already enough of a loser without having people find out I got cast in a huge movie…only to play a *girl*.

You couldn't pay me a million dollars to live through that kind of humiliation.

But I couldn't back out just right now, either. Not only would Mom be royally pissed off at me, I'd lose all potential chances of having my tongue roam inside Julia Glendower's very playful kitty again.

I could always back out later, right? Right.

I decided to play along.

I smiled politely at both of them, then got up and walked in the direction of the restroom, swinging the tote over my shoulder.

CHAPTER 3

IT WAS A BLUE OFF-SHOULDER dress. When I ran my fingers through the fabric, I knew that it was probably a designer dress. I'd never seen something like this before, much less touched it. As far as I was concerned, a woman's world was an alien world to me, and women's clothing and fashion was a very strange alien language.

I tried to figure out all the parts of the dress first. The bottom was poofy and the bust had an elegant bow, and there were diamond-shaped cut-outs trailing down on either side. I guessed that was where the hips were supposed to be. Along with the dress, there was a pair of midnight-blue strappy heels. The heels were in the shape of blocks and were about three inches long.

But that wasn't all that was in the tote.

My face scrunched up in disgust as I pulled out the final item in the bag.

A thin blue g-string.

No. Fucking. Way.

Heart pounding, I threw the garments back inside the tote and zipped it back up. I wasn't sure what kind of game they were playing with me, but I wasn't going to humiliate myself by wearing a dress *and* a thong in public.

I busted out of the restroom, and began my walk back to the table.

Julia and Terry were both laughing and enjoying dinner. Julia was looking like a dream, her seductive bustline on display and her fiery eyes sparkling. My cock tingled as I remembered her scent and the feel of her pussy folds in my mouth.

Did I really want to disappoint her? Possibly piss her off? Ruin my chances of eventually losing my virginity with someone so damn sexy?

Just because you wear a dress doesn't mean you have to agree to anything else, I thought. *Really. It's no big deal. You'll never see anyone else in this restaurant again anyway.*

"I'm not wearing a g-string," I muttered as I slacked my way back to the restroom. "No one's gonna know anyway."

Opening up the tote, I laid out the dress on top of the marble sink counters. I had to be quick in case anyone else came in and saw the weird guy in a designer dress in the restroom and reported him to security.

Placing the dress in a heaping loop on the floor, I stepped into it and wriggled it up my body, then did a few jumps in front of the mirror to zip up the back.

Digging into the bag once more, I held the g-string in my hand and shook my head.

I threw it back inside and picked up the heels. I scooped myself into them and instantly saw they were too big. How could a pair of heels be that big on me? Was I that small?

I sighed and walked to the large walled mirror that was flanked by potted plants. Of course I looked like a complete idiot. Why was I even doing this?

Pussy.

Oh.

I sighed again and went back to examining my reflection. That was when something dawned on me.

The design of the blue dress was apparently very deliberate.

The g-string was supposed to be seen through the cut-outs.

Fuck.

My plaid boxers were peeking through them, looking ghastly against the soft blue of the dress. So either I was going to have to wear the panties, or go commando. Either way, Julia and Terry were going to know.

Somehow, going out in public with my balls free and swinging seemed like a worse option than wearing a g-string.

Biting my lip, I removed my boxers and brought the g-string up my thighs. It had just enough surface area at the front to cover the entirety of my privates, but it was tight enough that I could feel the tension of the string in between my ass cheeks.

I bowed my head and walked back out to our table. I didn't have to look up to know that everyone was staring at me. A waiter almost bumped into me with a tray full of food, and I let out a small scream as I almost lost my balance. But the waiter kept apologizing and helped me put the heels back on again.

My face was practically on fire by the time I reached the table.

"Oh look, he's smaller than I thought," Terry said, surveying me with keen eyes.

"He's red all over," Julia said, her lashes sweeping as she took me in. "He's so *shy*. But then again, isn't that what we wanted? Wouldn't that make it more authentic?"

"I'd take authenticity over subpar acting any day," Terry agreed. He smiled at me, and his eyes raked through the cut-outs that showcased the side strings of the thong. His eyes widened. Julia's gaze followed his, and she licked her lips.

"Please, sit down, Jasper," she said.

"Uh," I muttered, slipping down into the leather seat.

"I think this little exercise has confirmed my initial suspicions," she said. "You look very sexy in women's clothing."

Sexy? I blushed hard. No one had ever called me that before.

"What about his voice?" Terry interrupted.

Julia waved the question away with her manicured hand. "I've already tested that out. He's got a naturally high voice for his age, which means he shouldn't have any trouble. He's got a sort of melodic quality to it as well, which should translate well on the screen."

I swallowed. They were talking in riddles! Why were they so interested in making me into a woman? There was no way I was going to star in a screen wearing women's clothing, that was for sure.

I'd had enough of this. "Mrs. Glendower," I said, clearing my throat while I spoke to make sure it didn't sound as high as they thought I did. "Could I ask about the role?"

"Of course you can," she said. "Terry, why don't you explain the whole thing to Jasper?"

"You can think of this as Jules's passion project," Terry said. "It's been a few years in the works, actually, since she retired. Jules is ready to have an audience again. It's just that she's been waiting for the right person to come along."

"Mrs. Glendower, you'll be acting again?" I asked, confused but also amazed as fuck.

"Something like that," she said lightly. "And if you're wondering about whether you'll be playing the role of a woman, no, Jasper, you won't. Though I know that even if that was needed, *you* wouldn't refuse, would you? I know you'd do *anything* for me." She smiled sexily.

I looked at her. All of my previous reluctance melted away.

I *really* wanted to please her.

"Jasper, we'll be doing a preliminary test shoot at my cottage which is a two-hour drive from here. It'll just be you and me though. You'll learn more about the role then, and I'll see if you're truly ready to take it on." She leaned forward and her palm grazed my thigh through the slit of my dress. She looked down at my body and I shivered. Why was she looking at me like I was a hot piece of meat?

"But I want to make one thing very clear," she continued. "I don't want just anyone. You have to give all of yourself to this role. If you're not prepared to do that, I'd like you to get the fuck off this table right now."

I froze. Seeing the anger flash in her eyes had fired something in me. It was so sexy.

Julia and me in a cottage alone?

I admit. At that moment I acted more with my dick than with my brain.

"You won't be disappointed, Mrs. Glendower," I said.

She leaned back and lifted her hand away from my thigh. I wanted to scream and tell her to touch me again. It was like I was under a spell, and I didn't give a damn about myself. She could've told me to get down on my knees and bark like a dog and I would've done it.

"Now, I'll be off to an event in the morning," she said with a satisfied smile. "But I'll be at the cottage soon after it's done. Let me give you the address."

I typed the address into my phone and then she handed me a key from her handbag.

"That'll get you in," she said.

"I'll be there," I said, fingering the key and smiling like an obedient puppy.

CHAPTER 4

JULIA'S 'COTTAGE' TURNED OUT TO BE more like a mansion set just minutes away from the beach. I arrived there early. The sun was still rising into the sky and it was dead quiet, with a nice, warm breeze heading toward the cottage from the waters. I'd taken my mom's car, which she'd let me borrow as soon as the words 'test shoot' had come out of my mouth. It had all sounded so glamorous to her, though I'd conveniently left out the part where I'd been asked to wear a woman's dress and a g-string for the audition. Oh, and the part where I'd serviced Julia under the restaurant table. I left that part out too.

I hadn't given them a definite 'yes' for the role, and I knew I didn't have to say 'yes' either. I was just going to take what I could get today and then I could tell my mom I didn't make it. I mean, I could take up acting by myself after this, couldn't I?

Inside, the cottage was just about as nice as I'd expected. Spacious and immaculate. I'd never actually been to such a nice house in my life. Julia had been sweet to trust me with the key.

I ambled through the house. I counted six bedrooms and the

dining area had a twelve-seater. The living space had a real fireplace and a 77-inch OLED TV. I rounded back and headed to what I'd pegged to be the master bedroom. It was so clean it was hard to believe anyone had slept there, ever. The walk-in closet was full of dresses—expensive ones with fluttery sleeves and ruffles and fur. *I'd worn one of these yesterday.*

Heck, I'd worn a g-string.

For Julia.

Even though I wanted to throw up at the memory, my face was quickly becoming red-hot. The way she'd looked at me like she wanted to eat me had been so titillating. I just hoped I could see that part of her again today.

I found myself gravitating toward a chest of drawers in the closet. I opened each drawer one by one, and was disappointed to see they held some pretty boring items: jewelry sets, boxes of makeup, and more jewelry. Except for the bottom one. That one was locked.

I calmly walked back out to the room. I had plenty of time to figure this out.

Fifteen minutes later, I held another small key in my hand. I'd found it right underneath a figurine on the nightstand.

I fitted it in through the hole of the drawer and it clicked instantly.

Bingo.

I wasn't sure what I'd expected to see in there. But it definitely wasn't a cougar's massive dildo collection.

It looked like it belonged to a damn museum.

I picked one up and ran a fingertip across the shaft. It was dark chocolate brown with veins criss-crossing through it and had a pair of giant balls. I was already rock hard. Just imagining that huge brown helmet head plunging into Julia's wet pussy.

Without thinking, I put the dildo into my mouth. The plan wasn't to suck a cock. It was to taste her pussy again. And in that second, I believed I *could* taste her.

"Oh fuck, Juliahhh…" I moaned, cupping my growing cock as I furiously pumped the dildo in and out of my mouth. "Will you let me fuck you? Just like this? Oh yes, I can eat your fat sexy pussy first. Mmm. You're fucking delicious, Julia…"

The sound of a car engine shot through the house. I let out a startled cry and wiped down the dildo on my jeans then threw it back into the drawer. I *couldn't* get caught like this. Not when Julia trusted me so fucking much.

I locked the drawer, closed the door as quietly as I could and rushed downstairs just in time to see a taxi sliding off down the road.

Julia stood on the paved stone adjusting her gold-rimmed sunglasses, an enormous handbag looped through her arm. She was wearing a tight cotton dress that went down to her knees, her gorgeous neckline and DD cups illuminated by some very colorful embroidery.

"When did you get here?" she asked.

"About an hour ago," I said, trying not to pant.

She handed me her bag. "Hmm. That's a long time to sit around doing nothing, Jasper. What *did* you do?"

I froze. The smell of my own saliva as I drooled over her dildo was still fresh on my mind. "I…nothing. Just played on my phone."

"I see," she said. She took off her glasses and her eyes scowled in disapproval when she looked at me. "You look ridiculous. Let's change you into something a little more fitting."

We went back upstairs again. I couldn't help but admire her silhouette and the contour of her ass as she gracefully walked up those steps in that tiny dress. When we reached her bedroom, I looked around stealthily like it was the first time I'd ever seen the room. My heart was skipping and fluttering when it dawned on me that Julia and I were now alone in her room with that plush queen size bed calling to us. I wanted so badly to make a move on her, but my cowardly virgin side wasn't about to let me have that freedom. I was too scared to fuck it up.

So I waited, letting her take the reins.

Julia waltzed into her closet and hummed while she raked her hands through her clothes. She skipped all the dazzling gowns and evening dresses and stopped at what looked like her nightwear collection. Her eyes lit up.

Oh no.

She took out a nightdress. The top was black and pretty much a bra. The bottom was red, although dangerously see-through, and flared out like a short skirt. It was something I would've expected my future wife to wear on our honeymoon or something.

Speechless, I just stared at the dress and then down at my old jeans and T-shirt. Then I locked eyes with her.

Julia shrugged and tossed away the wooden hanger. "I'm a lady of dignity, Jasper. I don't have men stay over here," she said crossly. "Did you expect me to have men's clothes just lying around? At least this is much better than the crummy outfit you've got on." She went through one of her drawers and pulled out a pair of red lacy panties. "This babydoll nightie is slightly transparent though so here's something for you to wear underneath. I don't want to see your goods. Not yet, anyway."

I kept staring at her.

She stared back at me, a very deliberate smile creeping up her face. Then she pointed to the door on our left.

"The bathroom's in there," she said flatly.

Pussy, I thought. *You're doing this for pussy.*

I went to the bathroom and locked myself in there, and put on the nightgown-lingerie thing. I was practically naked, and that's exactly what it felt like since the nightie barely weighed anything. Seeing my protruding cock underneath the flared red bottom was pretty jarring. I quickly put on the panties, trying to avoid how nice the lace felt on my skin. Women didn't wear clothes, I realized. They wore clouds.

Keeping my line of vision straight so I could avoid looking into the mirror, I walked out of the bathroom.

Julia didn't even bat an eye. She let out a soft yawn. "My event was a little hectic. I need a hot bath first." She grabbed a towel off the shelf in the bathroom and turned her back to me. "Will you unzip me?"

All the blood in my body rushed to my heart. I took a couple trembling steps forward and pulled at the zipper, gently bringing it down. Her back looked so soft and flawless and she had two dimples at the top that I thought was adorable. As more and more of her body revealed itself to me, I'd stopped breathing. The curve of her waist and the wider part of her hips was so sensual. So *womanly.*

I stepped back reluctantly when I was done with the zipper.

26

Tossing her head behind at me with a dreamy smile, she kept her back to me as she shrugged the dress off her body. It fell to her feet. With a quick push and pull, she sprung open the hooks of her bra, letting it drop to the floor. Her fingers trailed down and hovered right above the waistline of her panties.

Then she...she completely undressed.

CHAPTER 5

"EARTH TO JASPER! Have you never seen a woman's body before?"

Julia had turned around and was snapping her fingers, registering my reaction with a smirk on her face. Her braless breasts rocked unabashedly in front of me, her nipples as hard as pebbles.

I was mesmerized by her nudity. I bit my lip, wondering whether I should be honest about the fact that I was a 25-year-old virgin. That I'd never even seen a naked woman before. Not in person.

Julia laughed and skipped to her vanity, her big breasts bouncing. She sat down and began brushing her hair. I bathed myself in her frontal view, my pole swelling underneath my panties. I'd forgotten I was even wearing a babydoll nightie, and at that moment I didn't even care. I was so happy that Julia was letting me appreciate the most sacred parts of her.

Seeing a woman in the flesh was a totally different experience from seeing them in porn. Like, I could see that Julia's tits were natural because they hung a little low and the nipples pointed down, though they definitely didn't look like they belonged to an almost sixty-year-old. I could see her areolas were dotted with knots and had an entire valley of texture. Her stomach had a small pooch that padded out adorably as she sat.

I could see every scar, every roll, every imperfection on her, and somehow that was a thousand times more satisfying.

Julia set aside her hairbrush and gave me a sexy pout. I knew she was enjoying me watching her.

Enjoying the power she had over me.

"Seeing my négligée on you is very exciting." Her voice had suddenly gone all raspy. "I don't think I'll be able to stop myself from touching you."

She stood up and bounced toward me. I kept my eyes on her beautiful maternal breasts. "I know you're attracted to me, Jasper. You really enjoyed tasting me yesterday, didn't you?" She laughed and then her hand was on my stomach. Her touch heated my sheer nightie and my poor cock flinched. "How weird! I've had all kinds of men throw themselves at me. Very successful men. I even had a fan who was a prince from Dubai offer to pay me a million dollars to spend the night with him. He was so handsome. But I rejected him, Jasper. I turned *everyone* away because they just weren't doing it for me anymore."

My breath hitched. Because her hand was trailing down to my bulge. My big, blossoming panty bulge.

"Why so silent, Jasper?" she whispered. "Come on, it's just us in here. We can afford to get a little loose."

"I'm a virgin, Mrs. Glendower."

The truth had just blurted out. I hadn't been planning to be honest with her at all. But my body apparently had other ideas. It wanted to be vulnerable with her, to bare my real self even though it could take a bite out of my dignity.

Julia's hand retreated like she was in shock. "I would've never guessed you were a virgin," she said. "Well, that puts things into perspective, doesn't it? No wonder you looked like I'd electrocuted you when I asked you to undress me..."

I gave her a shy smile.

I was desperate for her to make another move.

Her hands landed on my stomach again. Touching all over. My stomach, waist, the side of my hips. Exploring my feminized body. She sighed as she lifted up the nightie and inspected my bulge. "I love seeing cocks in panties. Something about it is so exciting, you know?" she said. "So taboo. So intimate. A man wouldn't want to be in panties for any woman. He needs a really special woman to bring out his feminine side. Like *me*. Wouldn't you agree, baby, that your cock looks pretty in those red hot panties?"

I murmured some gibberish because my brain was fried. I looked down to see she had cupped my cock through the fabric and was slowly starting to massage it.

I was dripping pre-cum. I wanted to moan out loud but I couldn't. Was there anything nicer than a sexy woman massaging your privates? No. No, there wasn't. I was in heaven and hell at the same time, scared shitless but also unspeakably aroused, so aroused I could feel my inhibitions drifting away from me...

"I'm so glad you told me you were a virgin," Julia murmured and I blushed harder.

And then it happened.

She stopped her massage and I looked down. At the huge wet spot of cum.

I wrenched myself away in horror. I was fucking embarrassed.

"Oh baby," she said, biting her lip. "Are you horny for my mature pussy? Are you ready for me to take your virginity? All while you're dressed in women's clothes? Like my perfect little sissy?" She started caressing my cock a little harder.

"You're so hot, Mrs. Glendower," I said, and then I gasped as she brought out my cock. She rubbed the cock onto the fabric and then onto her naked body.

A strange feeling came over me. There were these weird pangs in my chest and my heart was feeling really heavy. Was I having a heart attack? That couldn't be right. I looked at Julia and suddenly everything became clearer. I might have passed out but I wanted to stay strong for her.

I groaned as she rubbed my cock all over her pooch.

I reached out to jerk myself off.

"Don't touch yourself," she said sharply. "You'll only do what I tell you to do from now on, understand?"

Helpless, I nodded.

Julia fell back on the bed and widened her thighs.

Her slit was glorious. So wet...so inviting...

She called to me with a finger.

My heartbeat spiked up. My nerves were all over the place.

I swallowed, looking down at my tiny bra top and the rest of the nightie that floated as I moved.

Julia's intentions weren't exactly pure.

But something was happening to me.

I was falling in love with a cougar who was hell-bent on

degrading me.

Fuck. This is not good.

CHAPTER 6

I FELL TOWARDS HER. I WASN'T sure what to do with my hands so I just pinned my arms above her shoulders, trying not to get in her hair.

Julia took the tip of my cock and rubbed her nipples with it. She kept doing it until my cock stiffened up all over again and a trail of pre-cum stuck to each nipple.

"Does that feel good?" she murmured.

It felt more than good. I was just a pile of goo bending to her whims. My body was all hers. With her controlling touch, my shaft traveled along her velvet-soft breasts and rolled over the peaks of her nipples. I drew in a sharp breath, my groin tense with need. Every muscle in my body was screaming at me to fuck her *now*.

I tried to take my panties off while keeping my balance.

Julia's hand came flying and struck me on my wrist.

"You'll keep those on," she said sharply. She relaxed back into the pillows and widened her thighs once more. "You like wearing the panties, Jasper?"

I knew the kind of answer she was looking for.

"I like it, Mrs. Glendower," I said timidly.

"There's a camera inside the bench," Julia said, flicking her fingers toward the edge of the bed. "Get it for me, baby."

I slithered down the bed and opened up the ottoman. Inside, there was a Sony video camera with the strap already attached. I handed it to Julia.

She pressed a button and the recording light came on. She signaled to me to smile.

"What do you think of my pussy, Jasper?" she asked.

My stomach was in knots. She was recording this? With my face and everything?

"I asked you a fucking question," she said.

"S-sorry," I said. This was beyond humiliating. "I think your pussy is a divine gift from heaven, Mrs. Glendower."

Julia smiled, clearly pleased with my answer. "Would you like to fuck a 60-year-old pussy?" she asked.

"Hell yes," I said.

"Then tell the camera what a good little girl you are, baby," she said in a seductive voice.

"I'm such a good girl," I said in this horribly squeaky feminine voice.

"Mmm. Will you be an obedient darling who wears whatever I tell you to? Panties? A g-string like you wore the other day? A push-up bra? How about a sexy minidress that will show off your tush when you bend over?"

"I'll wear anything you tell me to, Mrs. Glendower."

"Good little girl. Then why don't you bend over and show your ass to the camera? I think you'll look so sexy doing that."

I knelt down and angled my butt to the cam. I knew she could see everything because the clothes were so sheer. Could she see my ass crack?

To my horror, my cock rustled and hardened even more. I was getting horny.

"From the back you look like a real girl, Jas. It's mind-blowing. You're a real girl who'd do anything to make me happy. A girl who loves to lick pussies and suck cock…"

My eyes widened. "Cock?"

She nodded. "You can't fool me, baby. You think a place like this isn't rigged with cameras? My closet easily holds some of the most expensive things I own. I really enjoyed the little performance you gave me on my dildo. The best part is I didn't even have to ask! You're such a natural."

My blush deepened. I wanted to die.

She lowered the camera toward my groin then brought it back up to my face. "You ever wished you could deepthroat a cock? You can be honest, baby. It's just you and me here. And the camera. Don't worry, he has a no-judgment policy." She laughed dryly.

"I…I'm not sure, Mrs. Glendower," I mumbled.

"Don't think I heard you right," she said sharply.

"I…I guess I've wanted to," I said.

"Wanted to what?"

"Deepthroat…a dick."

Her lips curled. She was mocking me. "Such a slutty sissy!" she said. "Take your clitty out of your pretty undies and show it to the camera. Show me how hard it is after wearing all that sexy lace."

"Clitty?"

"Are you made of concrete, bitch?" Julia said impatiently. She waved a hand at my cock. "Come on. Use your fucking *brains*."

I remembered the way she'd blown up at me last night at the restaurant. It was pretty clear Julia was used to getting what she wanted.

If only she didn't look so *sexy* while she was pissed off...

I chewed on my lip as I held my erection in one hand while I placed the other on the waistline like I was posing for Playboy. My cock twitched, sending a thrill down my spine. I didn't understand any of this. This wasn't supposed to turn me on. All of it was making me nauseous and horny at the same time.

"Why don't you finish what we started yesterday?" Julia suggested, opening up her legs and bringing her knees up. "Do you think you can make me cum this time?"

The excitement was almost too much to handle. I nodded to the camera.

"Come to Momma, baby," she said.

I crawled toward her pussy.

I wanted to fuck her so badly. I wanted to lose my virginity with her.

But Julia didn't let me position my cock anywhere near her cunt. Instead, she pushed my head down so I could lick her. I dove in between her legs, tasting her with ferocious energy.

She stroked my head while I serviced her. "We'll fuck soon, baby. Do you like Momma's milk?"

I grunted in response.

"Ew. Answer me properly like a *girl*, Jas, not a pig."

I looked up. "I love your milk, Mrs. Glendower. I could drink it all day."

She left me in silence again. I rolled up my tongue and started fucking her with that. God, she was *wet*. She was spurting out her juices, and it was impossible for me to lap it all up. The sheets were drenched.

"Does any of this seem familiar to you, Jas?"

I froze.

"*Dark Desires?*" Julia prompted. "I did a sex scene just like this with a younger man. Of course, I was just about your age then."

I nodded. "I remember."

I wanted to kick myself. I wish I'd never lied to her about her work in the first place. Right now, I didn't want to lie. I wanted to be honest with her and bare my soul.

I made a mental note to check out *Dark Desires* once I went home.

"Do you know how sex scenes like this are done?" Julia said in between moans. "It's actually the least sexiest thing ever. It's just isolated body parts moving stitched together masterfully to insinuate sex. And it's hot with all the lighting so you have to try your best to be cool. But putting on those performances would make me so horny. I'd often rub myself in my trailer once we were done with the shoot." She stopped recording and placed the camera on the nightstand. "But this right here? This is the real thing."

I stopped licking and lowered my gaze to her pussy. She was still spitting out a stream of her juices. I'd never seen anything like that before and I was in awe.

Julia collected some of her juices and smeared it over her nipples, gesturing me to go back to tasting her.

"After I retired from acting, I faded away into obscurity," she said. "It's such a cliché thing, but it really does happen to a lot of actresses. I almost hated going out, because people always talked about my past. And 'my prime'. Never about my plans or the future. As if I was a dead woman walking." She rolled her eyes and then she spurted some more. I lapped all that syrup straight into my mouth. "But then Terry got in touch with me again and told me that there was still a market for me. It turns out that people like watching older women in erotic films."

I stopped and sputtered. "You mean *porn?*"

"Not porn," she said curtly. "Erotic films. There's a difference. I told Terry I'd consider it if I could have creative direction. I'm older now, wiser, and the last thing I want to do is bend to another person's demands. *Especially* another man's demands. I was itching to create something special and that was my own. I've always been interested in training a sissy."

"A sissy?"

"A femboy, if you prefer that term," she said. "But I don't. I like 'sissy girl'. That's what you are right now." She nodded toward me and I glanced down at myself and my cheeks went red.

"Anyway, Terry's already made me a website and we've got members signing up from all over the world," she said, her blue eyes sparkling with excitement. "We've already got a few hundred subscribers, and Terry's projecting it'll be in the thousands before I even release my first video. The membership price is pretty steep, but this isn't even about the money, Jasper. I have enough money. It's a way for me to love myself again."

"That's deep," I whispered, and I fell even harder in love with her.

"I could've done my recruitment for the perfect sissy online," she continued. "But I'm a bit more old-fashioned in that sense. I needed star potential. Did you know that last night when you were walking in that sexy dress for everyone in the restaurant to see, people were looking at you? You were turning heads, Jas. I can tell people will like you on camera. Plus, your shyness is sexy. These things are all important. You have to be a little relatable, but also very easy on the eyes."

Julia's thighs suddenly clamped around my neck and shoulders. I kept my pace and energy going. I needed her to cum.

"So, Jasper, you'll effectively be a co-star. Just you and me. Wouldn't you want to be naughty with me? Show everyone what a naughty sissy girl you are?"

I nodded before I went back to licking. My jaw and tongue were on fire. I was exhausted, but I needed to keep going.

"Now, I know what you're thinking," she said. "Going from a virgin to an erotic film star is a big leap. But I know you can do it. I'll be training you. Let's see how well you're listening to my instructions. And then I'll make up my mind. I want to see just how much you can please. I'm about to cum, baby. Yes!"

She cried out as she orgasmed. Her thighs and calves vibrated along my back. I held on. Kept licking, kept fucking her with my tongue. I was getting good at this.

"Tell me you need me, baby," she said while she was still in the throes of her orgasm.

"I need you, Mrs. Glendower!" I cried. "I need you so much right now! I love you!"

"Oh *yes!*" Her head fell back onto the pillow and her eyes

fluttered shut, her breathing easing down. She only took a second to reboot, though I waited patiently. I'd done it. Though I'd practically drowned in juices, I'd made my woman cum.

"Mrs. Glendower? May I fuck you now?" I asked politely.

Julia's eyes flew open. She grasped my little pecker, which was hot and hard and throbbing. She gave me a delicious stare as she swiped the fresh wetness off my tip and held it up for me to see. Then she pushed her finger to my lips.

Reluctantly, I sucked on her finger.

I wasn't sure I liked the taste.

"You loved that, didn't you?" she asked.

"Yes," I murmured, gearing myself to fuck her wet cunt.

"Alright, Jas, why don't you start by fucking me nice and slow," she said. "And have your panties around your legs. It's important for me to see those panties."

Shivering with excitement, I gathered myself and scooted toward her. This was my moment.

After twenty-five long years, it was finally about to happen. The days I'd spent cooped up in bed, wondering, fantasizing, dreaming about how it would go. How lucky was I to have a beautiful, experienced woman to guide me for my first time?

And it was everything I dreamed of and more.

Her fragrant pussy opened up just for me. I could feel it tighten and throb around me, and I was so happy that she was letting me experience the parts of her I couldn't even see, just feel. Julia sighed as I fucked her again and again, a little clumsily at first, but then gaining confidence in my motions and rhythm. She sighed and moaned and lifted her arms around her head. Her plump breasts swung up and down violently each time I thrust into her.

"Do you feel your panties around your legs, baby?" she asked.

"Yes, ma'am," I grunted.

"Fuck me as hard as you can," she said. "And don't even think about stopping until I tell you to."

I fucked her as hard as I could. My ass clenched hard as I jerked into her depths again and again, sweat pouring down my face. Julia reached out and cupped my bra top and fingered the lace lining of my panties, her moans getting louder and more desperate each time. It was obvious that my feminine appearance was the thing that excited her, maybe even more than my fucking.

But I didn't care. I wanted so badly for her to tell me I was a good lover.

After a while my legs turned into jelly, and my iron dick was close to erupting when she stopped me. She turned around and shimmied her delicious ass for me. Then she let me have her doggy-style.

My insides lurched with need as I pummeled into her plush depths from behind. This was too good…

I moaned as I finally let go. The release was mind-blowing. Load after load, emptying my big twitchy balls into her hot babymaking recesses.

I felt Julia tense. Then she wriggled forward, letting my cock slip out of her, and turned back around.

"Did I tell you to cum inside me?"

My cheeks turned pink. "No, Mrs. Glendower."

"I thought so. Then why'd you do it?"

"It felt too good, Mrs. Glendower," I said honestly.

"Did it feel good, bitch?"

I recoiled at the insult. There was a pit at the bottom of my stomach. This wasn't what I'd wanted at all.

"Suck all of that nasty sissy milk out of me right *now*," Julia said. She grabbed me by the ear and pushed me between her legs.

I drank it all up. I hated the taste and I hated myself. I'd fucked up our dreamy lovemaking session by having to slurp my own cum.

"You're horrible," Julia said, her hand smoothing my hair as she watched me lose all my pride and ego. "Just horrible. You'll never please a woman. Not like this. You should be thankful you're a sissy. Just good at sucking and swallowing."

When I emerged out of the darkness, my face was sticky with body fluids, sweat, and…tears.

Julia saw me crying and I could see it had triggered something in her. She called me onto her lap and nestled my head in the crook of her soft, warm arm.

"Suck on Momma's tits, baby," she said in a hushed whisper. "Then you'll feel better."

She cooed and hugged me as I suckled on the tender skin of her breast and the tough nubs of her nips. I kept crying, but then I really did begin to feel better. Wrapped in the warm cocoon of Julia's body, her breasts squished into me, I felt safe.

When she finally let me go, she looked at me long and hard. I was a mess.

"You know what?" she said softly. "This won't do. You're not turning me on anymore. I think we need to freshen you up a bit."

CHAPTER 7

FUCK.

Julia had that look again. Like she wanted to eat me for dinner.

She pushed me out of the bed and into her bathroom. There was a bathtub overlooking a giant window. Sunlight was streaming through it and onto the pristine white tiles, reminding me it was still only noon.

"Right. I need you naked," Julia said.

I felt cold and numb as she stripped everything off me. I was scared again. Lost. I didn't know what the hell she'd got planned for me. I'd lost my virginity not more than five minutes ago and my whole world had opened up, but now all I could feel was shame.

I'd let her down.

"What are you waiting for, slut?" Julia said, motioning to the tub. "You know, if you'd rather not do this, I'll let you go. I can easily find someone else who's completely devoted to me."

I rushed to the tub and sat down. She filled it to the rim and I almost moaned as the water hugged me like a blanket. She dropped a bath bomb into the water which turned it bright pink.

"Wash your face," she ordered, handing me a washcloth. "Get all that nasty gunk off."

I dipped the washcloth into the sudsy water and rubbed it over my face until it was clean. Then she gave me a razor and a bottle of shaving cream.

"Do you know what this is?" she asked.

"Yes," I said hesitantly. "It's a razor."

"Well, don't just sit there looking like an imbecile," she said. "Use it. Do your arms first."

"But…" I said sheepishly. I was prepared to do all kinds of kinky stuff in the privacy of her cottage. But shaving? I couldn't help but think what my mom would say if I went home all plucked and hairless. And what about Russell, her boyfriend? He already teased me a lot.

"Go on, girl, we don't have all day!" Julia said firmly. She put on a fluffy robe and sat down on the tiled bench across from the tub. I think she was just a little cold because apart from her arms she didn't bother wrapping the robe around her body. Her tits and her stomach pooch still looked so fucking hot to me.

That, and the fact that she looked just about ready to kill me now.

I nervously slathered on the shaving cream and slid the razor across my arm. With a good dunk in the water my arm became unnervingly hairless. Julia instructed me to shave my other arm before proceeding to my legs, my pits, arms, and my stomach. The whole time I felt like I was making a big mistake…until she told me to stand up and shave my cock and balls right in front of her. That was when I started getting horny again. Maybe it was the fact that Julia was staring at my privates, watching me steadily remove clumps of my pubic hair. Maybe it was the fact that I was doing something so taboo to my body.

Julia didn't comment on my boner as I shaved. She just watched me silently. Like a tigress hiding in the grass, waiting for the perfect moment to pounce.

Before I knew it, though, I was done. I'd never felt so…naked. So girly.

And I hated how much it was turning me on.

"Out," Julia barked.

I got out of the tub and she asked me to towel off while she went and got me some clothes. She returned with layers and layers of clothing piled high on her arms. She made me put on a pink bra and stuffed the cups with stockings so I actually looked like I had a cleavage. Then she slithered on a hot pink thong up my legs. After that, she hooked on a corset, which she pulled in so tight I could hardly breathe. Apparently that was to create a waist. Finally, she slipped on a pink bandage dress over my head and arms and zipped up the back.

And surprise, surprise…this dress was sheer too, so you could see all the undergarments I had on.

"Wow," Julia said. "You're prettier than I expected. Do you feel like a girl yet?"

I blushed. I felt so desired yet worthless at the same time. I wasn't a twenty-five-year-old man anymore. I was a shy, young, helpless girl.

Julia groped my breasts and snickered. "My my, what big tits you have!" she said, her eyes lighting up as she touched my body all over. "Look how soft your skin is! Were you ever a man,

Jasper? I don't think so…"

I couldn't believe she was poking fun at my feminine frame. She was the one who'd asked me to shave. She was the one who'd done this to me. Why? I used to be a normal guy. Now I was no longer a virgin but I was getting aroused at things that definitely shouldn't arouse me.

Tears crept down my face again as Julia kept humiliating and shaming me. She ripped down the front of my thong and smirked. "Did you shave your whole dick off? It looks so small! At least you can be glad you'll never fuck a woman again! What? Are you crying, baby?"

Julia peered down at my tears. I sniffled.

"Well, that's settled then," she said. "Men don't cry. You're a girl! You like being all girly, don't you? You like showing off to me what a sissy you are?"

I nodded.

"Good girl. Now wipe those tears off. We've got more work to do for the shoot."

She thrust me toward the window and shoved my face into the natural light. She doused my face in makeup, slapping on powders and colors and a wine-red lipstick. Then she stuck on some huge false lashes and covered my hair with a wig cap. She pinned a shiny brown wig into place. She said that she wore it for one of her sets twenty years ago, and that I should feel honored she was allowing me to wear it. She also made me wear the same towering strappy heels I'd worn that night at the restaurant.

Once we were done, she got rid of her robe, letting her body bask in the twinkling sunlight. I found myself gravitating toward her.

Never had I seen someone so beautiful. I lowered my eyes and saw that her shiny swollen cunt was *dripping*. Because of *me*. All I wanted to do was feel it, lick it, pleasure it, and cream her cougar pussy with my sissy seed.

"Good thing I'm turned on again," she said, taking me by the hand to her bed again. She spread her legs and lightly slapped her pussy like she was warming it up. It made squelching noises. "I'm just a tad sweaty and I haven't had my bath yet. It's a good thing I've got my very own personal sissy, huh? You can clean me up."

"Can I run you a bath?" I asked shyly.

Julia rolled her eyes. "Where's the fun in that? You've got a perfectly functioning tongue, haven't you?"

"You want me…to lick you?"

"What do you think, sissy?" she said, and whacked me hard across my butt.

I sucked in a breath and tried to ignore all the throbbing that was going on downstairs. Julia raised her arm. She giggled as I tentatively licked her underarm. Oh god, the humiliation. I was a cougar's personal body-licker.

I kept licking, giving my Goddess a tongue bath. I did her arms, her back, her stomach pooch, and her legs. The whole room smelled of my saliva. Whenever Julia thought I was being too slow or leaving traces of lipstick on her she slapped me across my butt cheeks or yanked on my ear. I wasn't being slow because I didn't want to lick her. I was slow because I was scared to do a bad job.

"I think it's time for you to clean my ass," Julia announced. "How about it, Jas? Would you like to clean an old woman's ass? You're a whore so I think you'll do it happily."

"I'd love to clean your ass, Mrs. Glendower," I said.

"Get to it then!"

Julia spread her cheeks for me. I inhaled her scent down there. My tongue hurt and my mouth was dry after all the licking but her ass was looking scrumptious. I worked from the outside in, slobbering over her soft, plump skin until I reached the pristine valley of her crack.

"After you clean my ass we can fuck again," Julia said. "Wouldn't you like that, baby? You want to fuck, don't you, my girlie? Oh, look at you all blushing. You're so cute when you blush like that! If you clean my ass well, I'll make the sex extra special, okay?"

"Yes, ma'am!" I said.

I was already so excited. My tongue landed easily on her wrinkled asshole and I tasted her, this time from the inside out. Her asshole was definitely tight as hell, and I couldn't help but imagine how it would feel to have my cock inside it.

Could anal sex be in the cards today?

Yes, I decided. My face grew pinker at the thought.

"God, I can cum just from you doing this." Julia moaned, sighing happily. "Nothing better than a sissy tongue up your ass. I swear, it's better than a cock."

I cleaned and serviced her ass until she'd had enough. My tongue and jaw were both numb, and I think the smell of ass became permanently ingrained in my brain.

"Now," she said, spreading her legs on the bed again. "I think you look so girly now that you can't fuck me."

My face fell.

"I'll have to fuck *you*." She gave me a knowing smile. "Don't pout, baby. I think you were made to be fucked. To be totally honest, I don't think you were good at fucking. Your clit is small and I could barely feel it."

Julia swung over to my side and fixed my wig before reapplying my lipstick. "You better not cry again, girl. I don't want your makeup ruined."

"Yes, Mrs. Glendower," I said in a small voice.

"Now hike up that dress and pull down the thong," she commanded. "Then bend over and show me your ass."

CHAPTER 8

HOW COULD ONE WOMAN HOLD THAT much power over me?

In less than two days, Julia had me wearing a daring dress, a g-string, bra and panties, a corset, a fucking *wig*. She'd stripped me of my masculinity. Reduced me to a freaky, kinky whore. I'd eaten my own cum and dedicated myself to licking her body clean. Now I was shaved to the bone, decked in lingerie and a tight sexy dress, baring my smooth, shaved ass for her pleasure.

And now I was about to get fucked from the back...

There was a sudden flash and my fingers twitched on my cheeks. I was straining to keep my ass open. I turned around and gulped when I saw Julia holding the camera and taking shot after shot of my brown eye.

"Just warming you up," she said cheerily. "I know you like to show off for the camera, don't you? That's right. Maybe we can use these shots as promo material on the site. What do you think? Keep stretching those cheeks. Wow, I can tell your hole is so tiny from here. Do you think it's tight?"

"I'm...I'm a virgin back there," I muttered. I felt like my entire body was blushing. I thought about what my friends and Russell would say if they saw the pictures one day, and I shivered. I would die.

I'd been so fucking stupid, thinking that today was going to be the day I'd brag to everyone about how I'd lost my virginity to a hot cougar.

But now I'd stooped so low that it now felt impossible for me to recover.

"Not for long," Julia said. "How about you try and put a finger in there for me, baby?"

I was glad my face wasn't to the camera. I took a deep breath and placed my forefinger on the rim of my asshole. Exhaling slowly, I pushed it in. Julia asked me to go in as deep as I could.

"I'm…I'm so tight," I croaked.

"Tight is right, baby. Let's bounce those ass cheeks," Julia instructed. "Keep your finger still! Show me the slut you know you are! Let's hear them clap!"

I twerked my booty up and down with my finger up my ass. The blood rush to my clitty was immediate.

This is ridiculous. Why…is this turning me on so much?

"Done," Julia said. "I'm so inspired. Now let's take a front shot."

I swiveled to the front and there she was, still unabashedly naked, her big tits flopping as she waved the camera about. I could feel myself leaking. Showing my face in that video was just about the most degrading thing she could've asked me to do.

"Well don't just stand there like a robot. Strike a pose! I want everyone to know you're not a man. Or a woman. Just a pathetic sissy. Show everyone your slimy clitty in those slutty panties!"

I really got into it then. I couldn't really help it—I was so turned on. I kind of propped my head to the side and did a knee pop while I showed off my shameful clit. I had no idea if it looked good.

"And what did you just do for Jules, baby?"

I looked at the camera. "I ate your ass, ma'am."

"And?"

"I...I ate my cum," I said shyly.

"Say it louder for the camera, baby."

"I ate MY OWN CUM!" And my clitty swelled even further.

Julia laughed. "She sucked it right off me like it was her morning smoothie! Mmm. How about a cum smoothie, baby? Oh, the possibilities are endless." She clicked off the camera, messed with the buttons a bit and said, "I just shared that with Terry. You've turned me on so much, my good little sissy. I guess it's time for me to fuck you."

My asshole puckered.

Julia asked me to kneel on the floor and set up the camera on the nightstand. Then she bounced her way to her closet. When she returned she was sporting a flesh-colored dildo attached to a pink strap on her hips. She was also wearing heels. They clicked while she sauntered over to me.

It felt impossible, but this was the sexiest I'd seen her yet.

"Show me how much you worship my cock," she said, swinging it up and down in her palm. "Give it a kiss."

I kissed the mushroom head of Julia's cock.

Julia giggled. She was getting such a thrill out of embarrassing me. "Now I want you to suck it like the girly girl you are. Don't think about it too much. Just repeat the little performance you gave me this morning, okay?"

My mind was like scrambled eggs as she pumped her cock back and forth in my mouth.

What the fuck was I doing?

I gasped as Julia thrust into me so hard I felt the dildo tip knock the back of my throat. My eyes were welling up with tears.

Julia slapped me hard on the face, sending me whirling back. I coughed and gagged.

"The fuck are you crying for, bitch?" she said. "I'm teaching you how to deepthroat. If you mess up your pretty face you'll have another thing coming."

She handed me a bottle of lube.

"Slather it on there, nice and good," she said.

A blob of lube landed on the dildo. I spread it all over the head and then brought it down the shaft. I was shivering all over. I knew what was about to happen. I knew what this cock was really for.

And yet, I couldn't get myself to verbalize it. Not even to myself.

The dildo was in my mouth again. I rocked my head back and forth, sucking on it with gusto like I'd seen a million chicks do in porn. I tried to swallow more and more of it each time I bobbed toward Julia, trying to silence my gag reflex. She kept laughing at my attempts.

"You suck," she said. "Literally."

She grabbed onto my wig and kept me sucking then pushed me straight into her cock so I'd gag again. She laughed even louder.

"Get rid of the thong," she said. "And look at the camera while you do it."

Helplessly, I stood up and took off my thong. She snatched it away from me. The next thing I knew, she was pushing it down my mouth.

I whimpered to the camera.

"Can you taste yourself in there?" she said, grinning devilishly. "Your soiled little thong?"

I nodded. It was a terrible reminder I'd worn them.

Julia made me lean over the side of the bed and splay my right leg on top of the bedspread so the camera could have a close-up view. I could feel the warmth of her body as she came close, her palm pressing into one of my ass cheeks. Then I felt the wet, slimy tip of her dildo trail up and down my crack.

Her breath hitched.

I could taste her excitement.

The dildo pushing through my entrance was like a prick at first. Then all I could feel was this incredible, overwhelming tightness. I panicked and cried out—or tried to at least. Instead, I coughed and blubbered into the thong sitting in my mouth. My nails held onto the mattress for dear life.

My makeup was getting ruined whether I liked it or not.

Julia stopped penetrating me. She could hear my sniffles. "Stay still, baby," she said. Her voice had suddenly gone soft. She was stroking my ass with her soft hands. "I know it's your first time. The first time can be a little tough. Well, here's a word of advice. I'm not going to lie. It's going to hurt a little at first, but then the pleasure will take over. Soon you'll be begging me to screw your hot little ass all day."

"Okay." That's what I tried to say, but it came out all garbled.

I had a feeling she understood though, because she patted me on the back and went back to fucking me.

She wasn't lying about it. The penetration did hurt. Even with all the lube, it still hurt. But as she kept thrusting and the cock further invaded my back door, I began to feel the force and the friction and the wetness of it all at once, and I was amazed by how good it was all starting to feel. Like, I didn't even know my body could produce this kind of pleasure…

I was huffing, puffing, groaning…all while Julia fucked me with the strength and energy of grizzly bear. The brown hair of my wig swayed back and forth as she pumped into me harder, harder, harder.

"Bounce that ass, baby," Julia growled. "Bounce while I fuck your tight virgin pussy."

My cock was growing. My balls were aching.

I desperately wanted someone to touch me down there.

I seized my cock with one hand and tried to jerk myself off.

"Hands off the squirter!" Julia blasted at me.

Her cock slid straight out of my ass.

"No!" I screamed, my voice muffled.

Julia grabbed my chin and glared at me. "You want me to fuck you? Well you'll have to beg for it now, sissy. How bad do you want it?"

I blubbered something.

"The camera can't hear you," she says. "Say you need me to fuck your tight little virgin sissy pussy."

"I need you to fuck my tight little virgin sissy pussy," I blurbled through the thong.

"Clap your cheeks for me," she said.

Saliva poured down my mouth as I clapped my cheeks in position, tears streaming down at the destruction of my dignity. She wrenched the panties out of my mouth, then bent down to drool into my own pool of saliva.

"Drink all of that up," she said. "Think of it as practice for your cum smoothie."

This is so humiliating, I thought.

I lapped up the whole pool of spit.

"Open your mouth," Julia said. "And angle it to the camera."

When I did, she coughed up and spit straight into my mouth. I swallowed it all down like a good whore.

She patted the top of my head. "I've trained you well."

The pleasure was almost too much to handle as she drilled into me again. Her cock stretched me to a capacity I never knew I had. I was experiencing what I could only describe as bursts of ecstasy spiking up my body. My crotch felt like it was being split in two.

Julia fucked me even harder.

I howled as ropes of cum ejected out of me. My entire body froze as I kept spurting, my asshole still clamped tight around the dildo. I bounced back to the dildo-head like a crazed whore, trying to screw myself in an attempt to milk every last bit of my orgasm, crying and screaming in my anguish.

"Beautiful," Julia said. "That was just a beautiful performance. You know what to do right now, don't you, sissy?"

I bowed down to shamefully lap up my fluids.

As soon as I was done, Julia hurried over and stopped the recording. She removed the harness and wiped the light sheen of sweat that glowed on her face. Even though she'd practically been through a workout the whole day, her makeup was still flawless and she looked beautiful.

"You're just perfect for the role, Jasper!" she said. "Thousands of people all over the world are going to witness our erotic films. Which means you're going to be a star! Could you run my bath while I call Terry? Hey, maybe you could call your friends and family and tell them the good news, too?"

"Uh, sure, Mrs. Glendower," I said.

I went to the bathroom and ran a bath. I took my phone from my jeans still lying on the floor and glanced over at my phone. No notifications. Except a text from my manager demanding an explanation for why I missed my shift.

I sighed.

The call could wait.

Julia took a long bath and then I stayed in the bathroom, bringing her various lotions and creams as she called for them and massaging them onto her skin. She did her hair and her makeup while I watched.

I found myself licking my lips.

Julia's phone rang and she answered it. I knew at once it was Terry.

"Filming starts on Monday!" she said once she hung up. She was beaming. "We need to go shopping. Get you some new lingerie and a proper wig! Some nice heels and a few good bras too. There's so much to do! A co-starring role isn't as easy as you think, Jasper. You'll see." She looked over at me thoughtfully. At my messy hair, stained face, and sweaty bandage dress. "Why don't you stay over? We'll have the whole weekend to ourselves. You need lots of practice, after all."

She waltzed into her walk-in closet and I followed. "Maybe we should head to the beach first to cool down a bit. Grab a bite on the way there. How does that sound?"

I swallowed. I couldn't wait to start filming. I wasn't sure what I was going to tell my mom or my friends. How they were eventually to see me on a screen playing a very…sexy…role. But somehow, that was a problem that seemed to be a long way off in the distance.

After all, didn't I have the whole fucking weekend to figure it out?

"Well?" Julia pressed impatiently. "I asked you a question, sissy."

I gave her a shy smile. "I'd love to, Mrs. Glendower."

THE END

SISSIES IN HEAT
MY WIFE'S NEW LOVER

MY WIFE'S NEW LOVER

CHAPTER 1

THE DAY MY WIFE TOLD ME OUTRIGHT that I wasn't satisfying her sexually was the day my whole world came crashing down. Allie and I are both thirty and have been married for a little over three years. We started dating in college, and by that time she'd definitely gone around and had quite a few flings and sexual partners. Allie was my first girlfriend and is the only person I've ever slept with. I wasn't even sure what she ever saw in me—a nerdy guy with shaggy hair and zero charisma—when she had a never-ending line of guys ready to give her anything she ever wanted. But she was adamant that she *did* want me, and eventually she even fell in love with me, and that was how I ended up tying the knot with a woman who was tragically out of my league.

Our sex life has always been complicated. Allie is extremely sexual and goes through cycles where she wants to be the one to dominate and then also be dominated. Being the submissive partner comes easy to me, I just hand her the reins and go with the flow. But when she wants me to be dominant, that's when all hell breaks loose. She wants me to tie her up and be extremely rough with her and call her a slut and other degrading stuff. And once she starts, she wants me to keep going…and going…and going…

Not only do I suck at all of that, I fuck things up so bad she ends up with the dreaded 'ick'. When the 'ick' happens, it's over for a few days and she doesn't even talk to me because she finds me disgusting. In the beginning of our relationship, Allie thought my lack of experience was cute and she was willing to teach me. Over the past year or so, however, it looked like she'd lost all patience for me and things were going south, fast.

That day, Allie and I had made love. I'd put her in handcuffs, kissed her pussy and used a vibrator on her for what felt like hours, but I hadn't been able to last once I was inside her. Normally Allie would head to the bathroom right after, but this time she just lay in bed with her legs splayed and my spilt seed still shining in between her thighs.

"You haven't given me a good orgasm in months," she said.

There it was. She'd finally voiced it. I was a crummy husband who didn't even know how to fuck his wife.

"I'm sorry," I said, bending down to kiss the top of her thighs. "I know I've been shit. I'll get better. I promise."

She crossed her arms. "No you won't," she said. "That's what you always say. I've had enough. Something needs to change."

"What?"

"I don't know," she said, getting off the bed. She was shouting now. "I don't have all the answers, Jacob. How about you use your brains for once?"

She slammed the bathroom door so hard the apartment walls shook. She came out a minute later and got dressed in a tight crop top and leggings, then gathered her dark hair up in a messy bun. She slid on her coat and began zipping it up.

"I need some time to think this over," she said.

My heart froze. "Don't leave," I begged, following her to the front door. I still wasn't sure how the situation had escalated so quickly. I'd never seen Allie so pissed off and unhappy all at once. Clearly I'd triggered her and I was too dumb to figure out how.

"Where are you going? It's almost midnight," I said. "We both need to go to sleep. We can talk this out in the morning."

"I need some alone time," Allie said, and when I tried to hold her hand she flicked it off. "Don't touch me!"

Once she left I was an anxious mess. I wasn't big or muscly or powerful and my small dick (3.5 inches) obviously made things tricky, but what was worse was I had no strategy and couldn't keep it in long enough to actually give her some pleasure. Something that was supposed to be so intuitive was so difficult for me. It was like I didn't know how to be a man, and Allie had every right to hate me for it. If only there was a magic potion to grow my dick and keep me from nutting until I needed to.

How could I even fix this? It wasn't like I could depend on a vibrator or dildo forever. At some point, women needed an actual functioning dick in their vagina.

I called Allie. There was no answer. I had no idea where she'd gone or what she was doing right now, but she'd been super horny tonight. What if she'd gone to a bar and a pervy guy hit on her? What if she flirted back and things escalated to the point she'd cheat on me and he was able to give her what I couldn't?

My face burned with humiliation at the thought. Allie had a good head on her shoulders and there was no way she would cheat on me. Not even when I'd given her unforgivably lackluster sex for months and she was horny beyond all reason right now.

Right?

I texted her in a panic, but didn't get anything back. I called her again, and again, and again. I messaged her one more time. She was giving me the silent treatment, which meant she was royally pissed off at me and I would be simmering in the aftermath for days.

It was past one in the morning and I couldn't get the image of some big burly dude being balls deep inside her out of my damn head.

I fidgeted in bed, completely restless for what felt like hours, but then eventually drifted off into uneasy sleep.

CHAPTER 2

I WOKE UP TO AN EMPTY BED. Sunlight spilled through the windows and the sounds of the city honked and blared in the distance, but the whole apartment was deadly silent.

Allie hadn't come home last night.

Panic crushed down on my chest as I fumbled for my phone and called her. I was trying not to think about where she might be. I didn't want to think about her in another man's bed, probably naked, while the guy probably didn't even know about my existence or didn't care, or both. I just needed her home and safe.

This time, she actually picked up.

"Hey." Her voice seemed thick with sleep.

"Where are you?" I asked.

Allie laughed, or tried to. She sounded hungover.

"Allie? This isn't funny. Tell me where you are so I can come get you."

"*God…*" she drawled, and I just knew she was rolling her eyes. "Chill. I'm with Nessa. I decided to stay over last night."

I blew out the breath I'd been holding. Vanessa was her best friend. So Allie hadn't gone to a bar or a club, even though she easily could have because of how horny she'd been. My wife didn't cheat on me.

Unfortunately, Allie noticed my sigh of relief.

"What did you think I was doing, Jacob?" she asked. "Having mindblowing sex with a man who actually knows what he's doing? With a cock that I could actually feel inside me?"

I stiffened at her crass words. The images I'd tried so hard to push away from my mind crept back in again, and I felt my groin tense.

"Please. You know I'll do anything to make this right," I told her.

Allie sighed. "We need to talk. I've thought of a solution, Jacob. I'm coming home."

I made both of us breakfast while I waited nervously for Allie to come home. When the doorbell rang I dropped everything and went to greet her. She crossed the entryway and sat down at the kitchen table.

She didn't waste any time.

"The solution is…" she said. "I need a fuck buddy."

The kitchen went silent. I felt my armpits grow cold with sweat.

She had to be joking.

"You don't need one," I whispered. "Let me make it better. Please."

I got down on my knees and spread her thighs apart. Allie didn't stop me as I pulled her leggings down and placed her legs on top of my shoulders. I shoved my tongue into her pussy and inhaled her hot, sweet scent. There was nothing that I wanted more than to give her the pleasure she desperately needed.

"You don't need someone else," I repeated and gave her another lick.

"Yes I do," she said sharply and the next thing I knew she'd pushed me on the floor. "Did you know what Nessa thought when I talked things over with her? She thought I'd been way too easy on you. She said that if it was her, she would've gotten a divorce years ago. Think about that for a second, Jacob."

A chill ran down my spine. *Divorce?* Somehow, even in the worst case scenarios I'd imagined, divorce had never been an option. I pictured Allie and Vanessa giggling and talking shit about me the whole of last night. Talking about my deficiencies. Talking about how they could get rid of me so Allie could be with a better man.

Had things really reached her breaking point? Was I that…bad?

"So what do you say, Jacob? It's either this…or…"

Allie left her own thoughts unsaid. She didn't have to say them out loud.

"How would you go about finding a man to…satisfy you?" I asked. "Wouldn't that be risky?"

The words 'fuck buddy' had been too painful, but even what I'd ended up saying was like a blade to my heart.

"Not really," Allie said. "I don't think I'll have a tough time finding a man at all. Do you think I'll have a tough time, babe?"

I stared at her. At her seductive brown eyes, full lips, and gorgeous face. Her big perky tits and her wide hips curving down towards her shapely buttocks.

Nope. She wasn't going to have to worry at all.

Allie smiled and started gobbling down the pancakes I'd made for her. "How about you make me a dating profile?" she said casually. "You know I'm up for a promotion and I'm busy with the month-end project. I'd like to delegate the manhunting to you."

I didn't answer. Making a dating profile for my wife to find her a new man to fuck was a ridiculous request.

"Jacob," she said, refusing to look at me. "If you're not committed to fixing this…" Her shoulders slumped. Again, her voice trailed off.

My heart pounded as another, more sinister thought came to me.

You know what would actually be ridiculous?

Divorce.

My throat had suddenly become too dry to speak. Still, I coughed out what needed to be said.

"Okay. I'll do it."

CHAPTER 3

THE VERY NEXT DAY, ALLIE CALLED ME to set up her dating profile. I couldn't believe I was even helping her hunt down another man she could fuck. Just a day ago she'd been *my* amazing wife—something I'd obviously taken for granted. How could things have changed so quickly? It was so surreal, and even though I'd agreed to do this for her, I felt completely helpless.

Allie made me choose all the hottest pictures of her, including one of her lounging in what was probably the smallest bikini made by mankind. The point, she said, was to make her look like she was single and slutty, since this was 'just about sex'. All I could do was nod and swallow as I waited for all of them to upload. My stomach was in knots thinking about all the men that were going to salivate over those pictures.

After the profile was complete, I had to reply to all the messages she received and then pull together a shortlist for her to shop. She told me how hot some of the guys looked to my face and tried to get me to guess what their cock size was.

"What about him, Jacob? Don't you think he's so sexy?" Allie asked as I flipped through the photos of an Italian stallion with gigantic abs. "How big do you think *he* is?"

"Looks like a ten-incher," I said through a mouth full of sand.

"Wow. That's a whole seven inches bigger than you. Well, six and a half, babe, really. I want to be fair to you." She bit her lip and looked at me, and I knew she was horny just thinking about it. "That's going to make a really big difference."

The pit of my stomach churned with humiliation. Allie seemed intent on rubbing it in while we did this, and weirdly, seeing her on fire as she hyped up these strangers at my expense was doing something to my brain. Suddenly, all I could think of was one of these men claiming her sexy body and Allie having one of the best nights of her life.

I'd *never* be able to measure up after something like that…

It took her less than three days to make an arrangement with the guy she liked the most. His name was Malik. I already hated Malik. He was the complete opposite for me—black, tall, covered in tattoos, and ridiculously good-looking. He was a personal trainer and it showed.

Allie made me ask him out on behalf of her and explain the whole messed-up situation: that Allie was my wife and she was looking for a fuck buddy after months of terrible sex. I felt so small as I picked up the phone and talked to this big guy about my worst insecurities. Malik didn't believe me at first, but when I managed to convince him that Allie was real he was nice enough about it. He said he didn't mind chipping in to fuck my beautiful wife and help us with our sex life.

Allie was practically swooning.

The day was soon fixed for their first date. It was going to be on Friday. If things went well and they actually had chemistry, Allie would bring him home.

"What about me?" I asked sulkily when she told me her plans. Had she forgotten that she still had a husband? Was she expecting me to just chill in the kitchen while she fucked a guy on my own bed?

"You can hide in the closet," she said. "Or under the bed."

I spun around to face her so quickly I felt dizzy. "Really? Is that what you want me to do? I'd rather die than hide in a closet and listen to some random dude fuck my wife!"

Allie was silent for several seconds. Her lips were twitching, like she was trying not to smile or laugh straight to my face. My legs were suddenly jelly. I knew what she was doing. She was airing out all her dirty thoughts now that she knew I couldn't do anything about it. I was completely at her mercy, and if she wanted me to be holed up and humiliated in our closet while she had sex with another man, well, that was what I would have to do.

"Then you can leave," she said flatly. "I was being kind, Jacob. I thought that's what *you'd* want." She rolled her eyes when she saw mine widen with disbelief. "Oh, cut that out. Don't you want to learn how to up your game?"

I froze.

"I thought watching Malik would be the best way," she said.

I looked down at the floor. *Goddamnit.* Maybe she was right. "Why in the closet, though?" I asked. "Couldn't I just sit on the recliner or something?"

Allie snorted. "No way. Sorry. I don't want you to be a cockblock, Jacob. It's either the closet or nothing. But then I hope—for your sake—you can find a better way to upgrade your skills."

I swallowed. It looked like there was no way I was going to salvage my pride and ego through all this.

Allie had all the power over me, and I would have to live through the humiliation of watching my wife fuck this big black dude through the slits in our damn closet.

I wondered what other cruel plans she had for me.

Surely there couldn't be much else. What could be more humiliating than being cuckolded by your wife? *Nothing.* I had to be more optimistic. Allie would fuck Malik once and I would watch and work hard at learning his technique. Then I'd show off my new skills and Allie would be forced to admit I was getting better at meeting her needs. If Malik turned out to be a troublemaker, on the other hand, I was prepared to do anything to get Allie back safely in my arms. Even if that meant calling the cops on him. Either way, things would go back to normal soon and I'd have my wife back.

If only I'd known how *wrong* I was…

CHAPTER 4

THE WEEK SPED BY. I COULD SENSE Allie's excitement building as her date grew nearer, though she didn't say anything about it. She didn't have to say a word for me to feel completely pathetic. What kind of a man was I, to let my wife fuck a stranger right in front of me? It was my fault that things had even got to this point, and the fact that Allie was so much more enthusiastic about having sex with Malik instead of me spoke volumes. She wasn't even attracted to me.

When Friday came around, we both went to work, and when I came home I got a text that Allie would be running late, but I could get things started by clearing out some space in the closet. I swore to myself as I took out dress after dress and folded them into a pile. I'd been so naive. I couldn't believe I'd agreed to hide myself in there while my wife had sex.

What was I thinking?

Allie came home about an hour later and quickly hopped into the shower. I watched as she put on one of her most expensive tops with lace cut-outs, spaghetti straps, and an extremely low bustline. The skirt she decided on was a tight leather pencil skirt that had a slit all the way up to her mid-thigh. She spent ages on her makeup, laying on false lashes and several coats of red lipstick sealed with a sparkling gloss.

She was going all out for Malik.

"Want me to drop you off?" I muttered. I definitely didn't want to, but I had to show her I was at least trying to be helpful.

She stood up and adjusted her tits inside the cups of her top. "Oh, don't worry about it. Malik's coming to pick me up."

"Oh."

She looked at me and smiled. *Fuck*. Malik was going to fall for her. So hard.

"Let's set you up in the closet," she said.

"Now?" I said. "I thought I could jump in there right before you guys come back."

Allie shook her head. "That's not going to work. I want Malik to be comfortable, and I need to trust that you do what I tell you to do."

My head whirled as she pushed me in the direction of the closet. Did she really want me in there—probably for hours—before she came back home from her date?

But Allie had this stern look on her face that told me she wasn't going to be very happy with me if I tried to be difficult. I squeezed myself inside, and though I'd cleaned it out somewhat, some of the boxes inside were extremely dusty and it was making me cough. There was barely any space for me with the closet door closed. This wasn't going to be comfortable at all.

Once I was inside, Allie asked me to strip. She claimed it was because she didn't want me to overheat while I waited, but I could see she was lying through her teeth. She had ulterior motives, though she wasn't going to tell me exactly what they were. Maybe this was revenge for treating her so poorly. Or maybe it was her way of teaching me a lesson. Whatever it was, if she wanted me to feel rejected and helpless, well, she was succeeding.

Allie stared down at my naked body. My nakedness was even more humiliating now that she was all dressed up for her date. *God, she's too good for me.*

Her gaze lingered on my cock.

I blushed.

Was she thinking about how small it was?

How big Malik's was going to be in comparison?

"Please don't," I pleaded.

"Please don't what?"

"Don't look at my dick like that. It makes me feel…small."

Allie's gaze was like a volcanic blast on mine. "Isn't that what you are?" she asked quietly.

I was crushed. I didn't know how to respond to that.

She gave me a soft smile. "Arms up," she ordered. She walked in her heels out to the living room and returned with a shopping bag. She pulled out two brand new pairs of handcuffs. They were pink and furry.

"Huh?"

She swung the cuffs in front of me. She was sneering, and it made my blood ice all over. It was clear she had zero remorse for what she was about to do, whatever it was.

She locked my wrists against the railing on either side of me. I tried to rattle my hands to break free but of course it was no use.

I was going to be left naked and cuffed inside the closet while she went out and enjoyed her date with another man.

Why was she trying so hard to humiliate me? Did I really deserve this?

"Go fuck Malik!" I yelled before I could stop myself. "Go suck on his big black cock! Or whatever it is you want to do!"

Allie's palm came swinging out of nowhere. Her slap on my face gushed all the breath out of me.

I gasped.

"Don't talk to me like that ever again," she snarled. "You fucking disrespectful faggot."

The words cut across me like lashes from a chain.

"Sorry," I said meekly.

I felt like an idiot.

"I've had enough of you thinking only about yourself," she said. "I'm not fucking someone because I want to. I'm doing it because you've acted like my needs don't exist for so long and you haven't even fucking tried to work at it. So it's time to cut the crap and think about what I need for a change. And you better pay close attention, Jacob, or you won't really know what's coming for you."

She crossed the room to our bed and went through the work clothes she'd tossed on there before her shower. She picked up her panties, the ones she'd worn all day. It was an old pair of granny panties, the ones she put on more for comfort than style and also whenever she was on her period. Then she walked to the laundry basket and took out another pair that she'd worn out for an event that week. This one was much sexier, with dark red lace trims that stayed low and hugged her hips when she wore them.

My heart pounded as she came back to the closet. My neck was strained because of the position of the railing, and my arms were already aching.

Allie took hold of my chin and stuffed her dirty granny panties in my mouth.

"I don't need to hear you talk anymore," she said.

I let out a choked cry. I could smell her…taste her…and it was turning me on. I stared at Allie as she went through her shopping bag again. There was a fierceness to her that I'd never seen before, not even the times when she'd tie me up and dominate me during sex. She'd never called me a faggot, that was for sure. This wasn't just domination. This was degradation.

Allie had taken a big pink feather out of the bag. She began trailing it down my nose, my lips, and my neck. She knew I was ticklish. I squirmed as she brought it down my cock and began to scratch the crown with its tips.

I cried out through the panties again as the blood rushed down to my groin and I swelled.

Allie just ignored me.

Why was she sexually torturing me like this?

Allie swirled the feather around the curve of my balls and let it fall further down into my crack. She pushed it in between my ass cheeks. The whole time, she had her jaw clenched tight and her lips pursed. She brought the feather back up and brushed it over my very sensitive erection. I felt my cock spasm with need.

My arms trembled. I couldn't even look down at her.

I did take a peek, though, and that was when I saw she had something else in her hands. It was a pink butt plug and a bottle of lube.

Without saying a word, Allie thrust my thighs apart and snuck underneath me. I gasped again as she drizzled lube all over my crack. I was *wet*. Then I felt the bulb of the plug press against my back entrance.

"Ohmmmymmgod!" I gurgled through the panties.

It had entered me. The whole fucking thing had entered me. My legs shook and I chortled through my mouth again. I couldn't hold my saliva in anymore and my breathing was becoming ragged at the cramping from that big pink plug stretching my asshole.

"Calm down," Allie said, rolling her eyes. "It's just a tiny butt plug. You're pathetic."

My entire body flushed with embarrassment.

Was it really tiny? Then why did it feel so big? Allie could take my cock in her ass like a champ. Apparently her tolerance for pain was a lot higher than I thought.

Allie tapped me on the leg, motioning for me to lift them one by one. I was so weak by then I had to do what she said. I was even more turned on now that I knew she was just going to treat me like shit and enjoy herself while she was at it. She brought her sexy red panties up my legs and snapped them around my waist.

"We don't want your new toy falling out, do we?" she said.

My erection strained against the tight lace cloth. From the back, I felt the fabric thrust into the base of the plug, keeping it securely lodged deep inside my hole.

Allie drew in closer to me and wiped away a line of dribble from my chin. "For every night you left me unsatisfied," she whispered and petted my butt, her finger twisting and pressing down hard on the base one last time. Then she kissed me on the cheek and placed my phone on top of the railing.

"Don't forget this is voice activated," she said, pulling the granny panties out of my mouth half-way. "I'm sure Siri can help you out in case there's an emergency." Then she closed the closet door and locked it.

Darkness fell over me. The only light that sifted through was the lamplight from the bedroom.

I tried to cough out the panties and failed.

"Goodbye, babe," Allie said sweetly. "I'll see you soon. Actually, I guess you're the one who'll be seeing me. I'll probably forget you're even in there." She laughed.

And then...she left.

CHAPTER 5

I STOOD IN THE DARK FOR WHAT FELT like an eternity, trapped inside the closet. Every sense was heightened while I was inside there. I felt the dust particles fly into my nostrils and the firing pain in my arms. I felt the elastic of the panties tight around my waist and the lace against my boner, and every time I tried to move the damn plug just seemed to go deeper inside my asshole. After a while I was able to cough out the slime-covered panties out of my mouth. Inside the hot stillness, I waited some more. Then I kept asking Siri for the time. I'd never known time could move that *slowly*.

I shivered as I remembered that the worse of the night was still not over.

Allie was still going to fuck another man. And I was still going to have to watch it happen.

I imagined her at the bar, strutting up to Malik and laying a hand on his rock-hard shoulder. She would smile at him flirtatiously, and Malik would look up and down her body. For one night, my gorgeous wife would be all his and there was no doubt he was going to be a very lucky man.

I heard a soft click. My heart leapt up to my throat. I blinked. My eyes were struggling to focus through the wooden slits.

I saw the door to our bedroom slide open.

And I saw *them*.

At first I couldn't even make out Malik's face. Just his massive body swallowing Allie's as he kissed her. The sounds of their lips smacking and their tongue squishing made my stomach flip over. He was wearing a nude T shirt over jeans and white sneakers that looked a little too clean. In less than ten seconds his T-shirt was gone and I could see his tattooed arms slither menacingly across Allie's bottom. He gave it a hungry squeeze. His forearm was probably the size of my leg.

Allie was already moaning.

"I've never seen a more beautiful cock," she said huskily, and I saw her wrists move jerkily near his hips. She was working his erection. "My husband's cock is nothing compared to yours, Malik. I know you'll make me feel so good."

I swallowed. She knew I could hear her. So Allie didn't give a crap about my feelings. Hesitantly, I looked down at my privates. In the darkness, all I saw was a little stub protruding out beneath my panties.

She was worshiping that asshole's cock while she had me dressed in women's undergarments with my backside filled with a plug, cuffed to the closet railing so I was forced to watch and hear every word.

What a cruel joke.

I raised my eyes back toward the room. It was like a public trainwreck. I knew that no husband should ever watch something like this, but I just couldn't pull my eyes away. There was no more foreplay. Allie was pulling Malik to the bed and they both undressed until they were completely naked.

I heard Malik suck in a breath as he saw her body for the first time. My wife's beautiful body, open and inviting for another man's cock. Then they started fucking. It sounded more like smashing. My view was just of Malik's clenching ass, dripping with little beads of sweat as he rammed into her with the ferocity of a raging bull.

"Open up for me, baby," he growled. "Open up that sweet white cunt for me. Let me feel how wet you can get."

I shut my eyes and cursed silently. Why was I subjecting myself to this? I'd thought Allie and Malik would at least be a *little* awkward. But they were so completely comfortable, it was like Malik was her real husband and I was some kind of imposter.

"Oh god yes! Fuck me with your hot cock, oh my god it's so big!"

Allie's cries made my eyes fly open again. Oh *fuck*. Malik was looking after her, alright. He was giving her what she'd been craving for years. My cock stiffened. Why was I so turned on? I was so fucking pathetic. I tried to move, but all that did was shift the butt plug around. I cursed again. Did Malik know I was in here? Restrained and dressed in panties while he was in complete control of my wife?

A shiver of pleasure made a fresh surge of blood enter my cock. It strained against the stretch of the panties, and I couldn't deny that it didn't feel good.

There was something I liked about all this. And I was mortified.

"Be a whore for me, baby. Just like that, baby..." Malik murmured.

"I'll be a whore only for you," Allie moaned. "Could you fuck my ass now?"

My jaw fell open. I wanted to yell out 'stop!' but I knew that would only make things worse. I didn't want Malik to discover me like this if I started to scream at them. What would he think of me? Some kind of loser with a midget cocklette.

Allie turned and scooted over to the side of the bed. She gently coerced Malik to turn to the side too.

It was so I could see.

I finally got to see the monstrosity that was Malik's dick. There was no competition here, that was for sure. My pride—or whatever was left of it—quickly withered away as Malik smoothly thrust his dick into my wife's hot asshole. He could only put a few inches in at first before he kept spitting on it to help slide it further inside. Then he started smashing again. Pulling her hair. Slapping her ass and hips so hard they had turned red.

Allie, as always, was taking it all like a champ.

I whimpered. Precum was leaking out of me and into my panties. I needed someone to touch me so badly.

Malik stopped fucking. "What was that?" he growled. He looked around wildly, and then his gaze settled onto the closet. For half of a split second, his eyes met mine.

I clamped my mouth shut. My heart shot straight to my stomach. *No.* The last thing I wanted was to be found.

Allie giggled. "Probably a bird by the window. Or something."

"Huh." Malik curled her hair around his fist and pulled her head back to meet his gaze.

I shivered as the horrible truth descended on me like a boulder. I was scared of Malik.

Allie glared back at him fiercely, like she was daring him to fuck her ass even harder.

Malik shook his head. "You're making me lose it," he said. "How are you so hot?"

Allie bit her lip. "It's okay. You can treat me like shit."

Malik pulled harder at her hair. I saw her neck muscles strain as she twisted around. "I'll break you. I'll fucking break you."

She moaned as he rammed into her again. I breathed a sigh of relief, though it ended in about two seconds. Allie was loving every second of it and I was so ashamed that I still had a boner.

I lost all sense of time as I watched their bodies collide against each other and Allie rubbed herself raw while her ass got fucked. When she climaxed I thought I was going to ejaculate because my cocklette throbbed so fucking hard hearing her scream in ecstasy. A minute later Malik announced that he was close and swung Allie around. He shot his load all over her face. With his cum dripping down her eyelids, they kissed again. Slowly, they regained their composure and started cleaning up.

I couldn't wait for Malik to leave so I could get out of the closet. I wanted to jerk myself off so badly.

Allie got dressed in her bra and panties and Malik made his way to the door.

I exhaled slowly.

"Wait," Allie called. "I know you wanted to meet my husband."

"Oh yeah," Malik said. "Where is he?"

Allie took his hand and pulled him towards the closet. Her lips twitched.

No. She wouldn't.

I heard the click as the closet door unlocked. I whimpered helplessly. The bedroom lights flooded into my face, and I blinked.

Allie laughed. "Malik, this is Jackie. Jackie, say hi!"

CHAPTER 6

I WISH I HAD BEEN NAKED.

Naked would have been better than wearing my wife's panties.

I blinked up at Malik's giant form. He was at least six foot five and two hundred thirty pounds. And I'd been right to be scared of him. He was leering at me like he'd pounced upon someone he used to bully in high school.

He looked at me with disgust.

"I didn't know your husband was a fucking sissy," he spat.

Allie snickered. "I didn't know that up until a couple hours ago either. Turns out he makes a pretty good sissy. Wanna see something cool?" She twisted me around and brought down my panties. I could imagine the base of my butt plug glinting in the light. I was so ashamed.

"That's fucking disgusting," Malik said. He glared at me. "Is the thing mute?"

Allie laughed. "I think he's just shy. I don't think he's seen such a handsome man before."

I blushed.

To my shock, Malik reached out and grasped at my waist. He brought down my panties. I squealed. I'd totally forgotten how to speak. His huge hand curled around my cock, which was so hard even though I was so humiliated. The look of disgust was clear on his face. He just wanted to play with me, and Allie was clearly egging him on.

"This isn't a cock," he muttered. "That's a clit." He pulled on my cock. And then he roared with laughter.

He was still touching me. And I was so sensitive after all that teasing that I just exploded. My cum landed all over him, and there was a lot of it.

Allie gasped. "Jackie! How dare you spread your cummies all over this nice man's chest!"

I whimpered.

"Clean it up at once," she ordered. By the way her eyes glistened, I knew she was so glad I'd only gone ahead and humiliated myself.

"How?" I asked quietly, jerking my arms against the cuffs.

"Use your fucking mouth," Allie said.

Malik drifted closer. The disgusted look on his face was made even worse as I tried to lick away my cum. He was impatient. He pinched my hair and shoved my face into his chest so I could clean him faster. It was like licking a warm, throbbing panel of steel.

The two of them started talking like I wasn't even there, and I was probably as red as a beetroot. I didn't know what it was about Malik, but he zapped out all of my confidence.

"You know," he said. "The thing is good with her tongue. I'll give her that."

"Would you like to fuck her?" Allie asked.

Malik flinched. "Baby. You couldn't pay me a million bucks to fuck this creature."

"I can make her sexier if you like."

Malik didn't answer. He just snorted.

"How about next time? You'll get two for the price of one."

"Depends," he said. "She'll have to seduce me."

I wasn't sure if they were joking. They had to be. Allie just wanted to embarrass me. I imagined Malik's huge dick fucking me the way he'd fucked my wife. I cringed. Did my wife hate me that much? To make me have sex with another man just for her entertainment? Just because she knew she had the upper hand?

No, she wouldn't go that far...

Malik soon left. Allie uncuffed me and asked me to clean up the bed so we could sleep. Other than that, she didn't say anything. I didn't have much to say, either. Allie looked like she was in dreamland, trying to process the amazing night she'd just had, and I wanted to give her space.

The bed was a complete mess. The pillows were on the floor and our bed sheets were strewn everywhere. The room stunk of sex and man sweat. Allie went to the bathroom to have another shower. As I was cleaning up the floor, I came upon a pile of used tissues on the floor. I picked them up and I instantly knew what they were. I brought them up to my nose and smelled it. A prickle of excitement ran through my body, and my cock started throbbing again.

God, Malik's cum shouldn't be making me so horny...

But it did. And that was scary.

I'd always known I was a submissive guy, but not to this

extent. I thought about Allie asking Malik if he would fuck me. The cruel smile on her face as she joked with him about making me sexy so I could seduce him. With the grim way he'd looked down at me as I cleaned up my 'mistake', I knew he'd give me no mercy if he were to have his way with me. I'd be nothing more than a toy with a hole. Maybe that was exactly what I needed.

What was happening to me?

I'd never known Allie to be so vicious. She was enjoying the power she had over me, now that the threat of divorce was over my head, and it was doing all kinds of fucked up things to me. If only I hadn't been such a bad husband. I'd totally taken her for granted, and now it was coming back to bite me in the ass.

***

Allie finally came to talk to me the next night.

"You've been unusually quiet," I said.

"You have too," I said. "But sorry. I've just been…processing things."

"Well? What did you think about the experience?"

I hung my head low. "I know you enjoyed it."

"Malik was amazing. So sexy. So attentive. He gives me what I really want," Allie said. She raised an eyebrow. "But I wasn't the only one who had an orgasm out of it. And that was a heck of an orgasm."

I remembered blasting my cum onto Malik's chest and then being ordered to lick it off. I shuddered. That was only one of the humiliating things to happen to me that night, and I just didn't want to go there.

"Jacob? Does Malik having sex with me turn you on?"

I sighed. I couldn't exactly lie to Allie. She'd get the truth out of me somehow. "It's sex," I said. "Of course it turned me on."

"You know what? It turned me on, too," Allie said. "Not just the having sex with Malik thing. The thought of you watching. Making you totally helpless."

"Really?" I was shocked. She hadn't said I'd turned her on in...what? Months?

Were we moving in the right direction?

"I'm going to ask you another question, Jacob," Allie said. "And I want you to be totally honest."

I turned to face her and took a deep breath. "Okay."

"Does *Malik* turn you on?"

I wasn't sure how to answer that.

I mean, I wasn't sure of the answer myself.

I decided to be honest again. "He reminds me of what I don't have, Allie. He has a big dick and I don't. He's great at fucking. I'm not. You obviously find him attractive. And you obviously think I'm not...so..."

Allie smiled. "Well, you know the good news? I think you can turn Malik on too. And you know what, that would turn me on so much too! I can imagine you already. A sexy skirt, stockings, big fake breasts, a wig. In fact, I think you could be a better whore for Malik than me."

My heart just sank. The fact that she didn't even deny that she wasn't attracted to me stung like crazy.

"Why are you doing this?" I asked her in a small voice.

Allie didn't answer. She looked over at me, power glazing over her big brown eyes.

"Because I can," she finally said. The pure pleasure she had in making me feel small and tiny oozed through every word like honey. "Because I like seeing you all helpless, babe. Willing to do anything for me. At least that way I can tell that you love me."

I shuffled my feet. My dick was stiffening at the way she was talking to me. I'd always loved her. It was crazy to think she'd never felt that.

"So what do you want me to do?" I asked. "Tell me what you want and I'll do it."

Allie smiled again. My chest brimmed with love and desperation. I'd never felt anything so intensely before.

"I want you to pull down your pants and turn around," she said.

I didn't hesitate. She pulled my ass cheeks apart and then her finger was inside my ass. I groaned. She slathered some lube and inserted the pink butt plug inside me. She pushed it in hard until the whole thing popped into my asshole.

"I want you to sleep in this tonight. Can you do that for me, babe?"

Humiliated, I nodded.

"Here are some panties for you to wear," she said, tossing me the pair she'd been wearing. "Pull it up tight so the plug stays put."

She was silent as I wore her used panties.

"As for what else I want you to do..." she said. "I'll let you know when I want to."

Allie didn't say another word to me.

I gave her a defeated smile and got ready for bed.

CHAPTER 7

LIFE CONTINUED AS NORMAL THE following week. As normal as things could be with me wearing panties and a butt plug to bed every night. Though it never stopped being extremely humiliating, the fact that Allie was giving my butthole attention was somehow affirming, though she didn't seem interested in having actual sex with me. The butt plug, I realized, was the least I could do to please her. In fact…I could do more. I had to do more. I had to show her how much I wanted her. *Loved* her. Maybe…just maybe she'd even forget about Malik then.

One evening, Allie sent me a message saying that she was coming home early and she would like me to be there. I cut my shift short and stopped by the florist in the mall next to my office and picked up a bunch of lilies and roses. They were Allie's favorite flowers, and this was the perfect moment to be a little romantic.

Once home, I unlocked the front door and stepped inside, being careful not to crush the bouquet as I closed the door behind me. Then I stopped short.

I could hear noises from the bedroom.

Was Allie already home?

I trudged forward, my legs suddenly feeling weirdly heavy. And then I heard it.

Sex noises.

Allie was fucking someone in our bedroom.

Malik.

A lump formed in my throat. As I crossed the entryway I saw a big envelope labeled 'READ THIS' propped up at the kitchen table. Next to the envelope were…clothes. Women's clothes.

Sexy women's clothes.

"Oh god…" I murmured, picking up the envelope and ripping it open.

This couldn't be good.

Jacob, you asked me what I want you to do. I want you to wear everything laid out in front of you for me and Malik. Don't bother coming into the bedroom if you don't want to do it. We can have plenty of fun without you. Trust me. Love, Allie.

My heart went into overdrive as I took in what she wanted me to wear. All neatly laid out on top of the table like a big feast. Allie had kept her word. I saw a thong. Stockings. Heels. A skirt and a blouse. A baseball cap with actual *hair* attached. An open tube of lipstick.

My cock twitched. I couldn't deny that the thought of being made into a girl was making me feel excited…

Allie was being completely serious. I could still hear Malik's grunts coming from the bedroom. How could I confront them if I didn't do what she said? I was too scared.

I didn't have any balls.

You're doing this for your marriage, I tried to remind myself. *Not because you really want to dress up like a slutty girl. Not because your wife is dead set on making you seduce her new lover, no matter what it takes…*

Before I could second guess myself, I gathered everything up and went to the guest bathroom and stripped down. The sounds of them kissing and moaning floated through the walls. Every smack and groan was like a blow to the gut, but my dick apparently loved it.

I was so clueless I didn't even know what order to wear the clothes in, but I knew I didn't have much time to figure it out.

I put the thong on first because panties were the ones I was most familiar with. It looked like a brand new pair, and was comfortable enough except for the actual thong part, which kept riding up my ass crack.

I decided on the stockings next. They were dark enough that they concealed my body hair, which was kind of encouraging, though I wasn't the hairiest person. Because hairy legs would be the worst thing to happen tonight, right? Maybe this wasn't going to be so bad. I was just playing dress-up. And watching someone else fuck my wife. That's all.

The skirt went on next. It was a red plaid skirt. Also new. Everything Allie had given to me this time was brand new. She wasn't even making me wear her hand-me-downs. A pang of arousal went through me as I realized just how determined she was to turn me into a woman. That was strangely hot.

With the skirt on, I could no longer ignore the bra. Thankfully that didn't take too much time. It had to be a wonder bra because once I hooked it on I had actual, somewhat spongy-looking cleavage. That was the moment I knew I *really* looked like a slut.

I looked like a boy-crazy girl who was down for absolutely anything. Every part of this plan had been so well thought of by Allie.

One by one, I put the rest of her humiliation plan to motion. The white top that plunged low enough to show off the bra I'd been made to wear. The baseball cap, clipped on, that made me look like I had the hair of a Victoria's Secret model. The heels. They fit perfectly. Of course. And finally, the lipstick.

What had I become? My reflection told me I wasn't Jacob anymore. I had sex written all over me. The redder than red lips. The massive fake breasts, just barely concealed by my white schoolgirl top, probably could make any man salivate. Heck, they were making me drool. But all of this would mean nothing if I couldn't turn Malik on...

I gulped. What if he chased me out of the room? Called me names? What if Allie didn't think I still wasn't sexy enough?

Enough. It was time to make a move.

I cruised down the corridor—as gracefully as I could in five-inch heels. The bedroom door was open just a few centimeters. They were fucking, alright. Allie was squatting and jouncing on Malik's cock while his big hands smothered her butt. She was naked except for her thigh-high stockings and heels. Both were the same kind I was wearing. So she'd wanted us to match for tonight.

I crept into the room, and silently waited.

CHAPTER 8

AT FIRST I WASN'T SURE IF THEY saw me. I had to stand there like a complete cuck, watching as the bed—*my* bed—got messier and messier. I was so self-conscious, I could barely breathe.

Allie suddenly stopped bouncing and turned to me.

She didn't say anything at first. Just bit her lip as her eyes glazed over, traveling up and down my outfit. It was like she was drinking every inch of my body. My new hair. My gigantic breasts. My belly button popping out from underneath the top.

For the first time in a long time, I could tell she really *wanted* me.

Just when I thought Allie would say something to me, she turned back around and kissed Malik passionately on the lips. "Thanks for making me feel amazing," she said. "I love you." She began slowly gyrating on Malik's cock, sliding up then down so I could see his cock impaling her over and over again. His cock was drenched with her secretions.

She was horny beyond belief.

Malik reached out to kiss her again and their tongues twirled.

All while she was still riding him *verryyy* slowly. "God. You're so much better than my husband," she whispered. "You saw how small his cock was right? You were right. It's a clit. I could barely feel him when he was inside me." He nipped at her neck and she moaned. "And he can never control himself. Ugh. You have no idea how much you're fucking up my life. I don't think I can have sex with my husband again!"

I almost moaned out loud at her insults. It was cruel. So, so cruel. She really wanted to hit me where it hurt the most.

"Are you happy for me, babe?"

I froze. Allie was talking to *me*.

"Yes," I said quietly.

"Speak up, baby. What are you happy about?"

"That you found a man with a much bigger dick." I covered my skirt up from the front, terrified that she'd see my boner.

"Well, don't just stare at us like a dummy and be a mood killer," Allie said. "Come here."

I walked unceremoniously to the bed. My heart was practically in my throat.

"Say hi to Malik," she said, grinning.

She could tell I was terrified of Malik and wanted to rub it in. The thing was, I didn't know why I was so afraid of him. He did look scary, but I was also such a wimp. Maybe it was because he reminded me of everything I wasn't.

"Hey sissy," Malik said. He wasn't even looking at me. "What do I call it?"

"You can call it whatever you want," Allie said.

"Butters," Malik said to me. "You look like that girl from high school who sucked everyone's dicks but still couldn't get a boyfriend."

"You don't think she's hot?" Allie said seductively. "Not even a little?"

"Fugly face, but the body is a'ight."

"Lift up the skirt, babe," Allie said. "Show Malik your ass."

I did as I was told. I couldn't believe I was showing off my ass to my wife and her lover.

"Shake your ass," she said.

Again, I had to obey her. I felt my ass move and jiggle in a way I'd never felt before. I was being gripped by some very dark and very taboo desires, and I couldn't stop myself from being overtaken by them. Allie began slapping my ass to an imaginary beat, and I loved that. As her hands thundered down on my flesh, hitting me harder and faster, I just moved and bounced my ass more vigorously.

"You like that? You like showing a man your hot ass?" She was shouting at me again.

I whimpered and said nothing. Just kept jiggling my hips and bottom. Suddenly, I felt a hot brick lay down on my bare ass cheek. It gave my ass a good squeeze. My heartbeat went through the roof.

It was Malik.

"So would you tap that?" she asked.

"No, never," Malik said, and laughed like an ox.

They both kept laughing.

This was so humiliating. Was Allie really going to convince Malik to fuck me? He was so rough. Could I even handle that?

A chill ran down my spine as I realized I was really imagining riding Malik like my wife had ridden him.

What the fuck was wrong with me?

"Ready for round three, baby?" Allie said. "Jackie, give his shoulders a rub while he fucks me."

I trotted to Malik's side. I was too scared to even touch him. He was just so big and bulky. I swallowed and placed my clammy hands on his smooth, dark shoulders. *Good fucking lord.* It was like touching a giant slab of concrete.

Malik groaned as I began massaging him.

"I'm glad you're making yourself useful, Jackie," Allie said.

I nodded. I wanted to serve them in any small way I could— at least that way I didn't feel completely worthless.

"That feels good, butters," Malik grunted. "Keep doing whatever the hell you're doing while I bless your wife with my dick."

"I will," I squeaked.

My little fingers slid and slipped on his sweat-laden back as I continued to make him feel good. I didn't even need any massage oil. His skin was that good. This was the guy who had wooed Allie, dominated her, and made her fantasies come to life. I had to respect that, right?

I watched Allie fuck him until she was just about to cum. She just bent over and collapsed onto Malik's chest, wrapping her arms around his neck and whimpering with need. Her beautiful face was mere inches away from mine, her full lips red from excitement and almost swollen with arousal, a trail of bite marks all down her neck. I wanted to grab onto her and kiss her while she came in my arms. But I couldn't. She wasn't mine. Not tonight.

Malik grunted loudly and lifted Allie off his lap so he could thrust into her from below. I could literally see the soft wet pink of her inner pussy spread even more for him.

"Watch me, babe! Jackie! Watch me cum on his dick!" Allie cried out, her eyes clenched shut as she rode her orgasm.

This was too hot. With one palm on Malik's back, I placed the other underneath my skirt and stimulated my clit a little as I watched the show. I was wet, too. I touched myself because I knew I could only do this while I was horny.

"That was amazing. I love you, baby," Allie whispered.

"Anything for a chocolate-loving whore like you," Malik rumbled, and squeezed her butt so hard he left finger marks on the sides.

Allie's eyes glittered with excitement. "You'd do anything?" She turned to me, her eyes narrowing with suspicion at my missing hand. I slowly snuck it out and placed it back on Malik's back, having a sick kind of pleasure at smearing a little of my naughty pre-cum over his god-like body. "Would you be willing to fuck my sissy husband?"

I gasped. There was no way she was serious.

Allie rolled her eyes at me. "Don't act so surprised. Why do you think I dressed you up like a slut? Got you used to the plugs?"

"Plugs?" Malik asked, his brows wiggling.

"You saw it the other day, baby. Tell him, Jackie."

I felt shy all of a sudden. "Allie has been making me wear a butt plug every night," I said. "To stretch my back hole."

Malik laughed. "You're sick, Allie."

Allie pouted. Even though Malik was crazy dominant, she knew where the real power lay in their relationship. "My theory is the only way to teach him how to make love like a man is to have sex like a woman. So. What can he do to make you want to fuck him?"

"There's only one way I guess. The thing will have to seduce me," Malik said.

My ass clenched at those words. Seduce? *How the fuck do I seduce a man?*

"So, Jackie, it's your turn to tell me. Do you want Malik to fuck you like a woman?" Allie asked me. "Be honest."

The room swayed and swam in front of me. My body felt weak and rubbery. I was giddy with fear.

I wanted to think with my brain, but I just couldn't.

"I do," I choked.

Allie gave me the brightest smile in the world. She was getting some kind of depraved pleasure from seeing whether I could turn on a straight man. She called me to the bed and asked me to touch Malik's cock. It was so weird yet thrilling to have his cock in my hand. It had gone floppy again, but as I held it and slowly pumped it up and down I could feel it start to harden, though that was more down to Allie's sexy whispers to Malik than to my touching. Once it was getting hard, Allie ordered me to take it in my mouth.

"Suck it, baby," she said, swiping my long fake hair over my shoulder. "You know you want to!"

His musk sifted through my nostrils and I felt weak again. I knew if I wasn't so horny I would've retched all over it. But I didn't want to show Malik that on any other day I would've found his whopper utterly disgusting. Just in case he somehow got pissed off. So I let his man smells permeate my body and bravely started to lick him.

"Don't lick it, fucking *suck* it," Allie snapped in my ear.

She pushed me away and took hold of Malik's cock.

"Let me show you how it's done."

Allie proceeded to give him the hottest blowjob in the world. She teased him by licking his head like a lollipop before plunging the entire thing confidently into her mouth. Malik's groans and grunts soon filled the room. Then she handed it over to me. She'd just taught me something a wife should never have to teach her husband. I just gave her a look and her evil smile made my stomach quiver uncontrollably. Something about this was so wrong. So hot. When I tasted Malik again, his cock was pulsating excitedly on my tongue. Then Allie ordered me to choke on his cock, telling me that Malik would love it. So I did it. I slithered his penis down my mouth until I was really close to gagging and I left it to throb there for a while before letting go, only to do it all over again. Precum sifted through my lips and rested on my tongue, and I tasted it eagerly. *Goddamnit.* I wasn't a man anymore. My wife had turned me into a whore.

"Baby, it's time," Allie said sweetly. She was holding up two pink furry handcuffs.

I was quickly cuffed to the bedposts, my arms stretched out like two sticks of spaghetti. I was sprawled out, sporting a blouse and a skirt, my body handed over to a man who was built like a tank and had the sexual appetite of a starving grizzly bear. I had no control now. No control over what was happening to me.

Malik licked his lips. He gave me a smile, but the smile didn't reach his eyes.

I must've looked terrified because Allie patted me on the head and said, "Don't be scared, babe. I'm right here."

Malik snickered. "You ready, butters?"

I whimpered.

My chest heaved in the short silence that followed. Then two meaty hands grasped the curve of my hips and the sound of tearing fabric blasted my ears. Malik was practically ripping my stockings and thong to shreds. Cold air swept through my now completely exposed butt, and then hot fingers clawed at my skin, parting my cheeks and revealing my dark puckered hole. Those brutish hands squeezed my ass so hard it felt like he was digging straight into my body. His touch was so fucking rough.

The thought of Allie and Malik seeing the most intimate part of me sent shivers down my back.

I heard the emptying of a lube bottle and the brazen sound of Malik spitting a few times on his cock.

Then his slippery wet pole wedged itself against my rear entrance.

CHAPTER 9

THIS WAS IT. THE DESTRUCTION of Allie's husband.

I had been turned into a sissy plaything by my wife and now her fuck buddy and lover was about to rail me *hard*.

For once, my crazed mind had come to a halt. It was like I'd finally accepted my fate.

"Oh my god!" I yelped as Malik entered me.

"Deep breaths now," Allie said. "I won't lie. It's going to hurt a little. But you're a big girl now and I know you can take it."

I gritted my teeth and forced myself to take deep, full breaths. *Motherfucker. It hurts.* I clambered forward a bit and held onto the railing of the bed for support. The pain was more of a tight tension than anything else, and Allie's soft fingers were helping me stretch open. I let out a faint groan. As Malik slowly slid his way into me, I felt myself beginning to let go. All the tension was loosening up and my asshole was inviting a stranger's cock inside it.

"You like it, babe?" Allie murmured, her long nails scratching my back. "You like the big black cock in your ass?"

I clutched onto the railing harder. All I could see was red.

"He's in deeeeep," Allie said, more quiet now, as if she was completely mesmerized by the scene before her. "Oh god...oh god..."

The pressure was almost too much. Almost. I bit down on my tongue to keep myself from crying like a sissy.

"You look so sexy like this, babe," Allie said softly in my ear. "This is the hottest I've ever seen you. I'm so happy you're doing this for me, babe. Fuck. You're taking him so bravely. Such a good girl. Do you want Malik to start pumping now? Pumping your hot little pussy? Just for me?"

"Uh-huh," I whispered in a soft, girly voice.

"Keep that pussy nice and open, babe," Allie said. "Yes, just like that. Malik loves fucking you. I can see that. I bet you're tighter than me. God, how do you feel about letting such a handsome man fuck you? Do you think you can make him cum, baby? Do you?"

I whimpered like a helpless puppy. Her words danced inside my head. She was being so fucking dirty. The room swung back and forth as I gave up my asshole to my wife's boyfriend. I felt like I was slipping away into the crater of a volcano. The pull of pleasure and sin was too much. It was done. There was simply no coming back from this. Malik held me by my bony hips and fucked me like I was a doll. There was almost an anger to the way he was claiming my body. He was fucking me exactly the way I watched him fuck Allie. He grabbed me roughly by the hair, pulling on the clips so hard it made my scalp scream. My spine bent his way as he urged me to look at him. There was so much revulsion in his face. He hated me. He hated me so much because…maybe he liked it. Maybe he liked fucking a small, tight virgin sissy like me.

I stared back at him defiantly, urging him to take me even harder.

"Look at you babe," Allie said. She had her horny voice out now. "You love this. I knew you'd love this! Tell me how much you want this, babe…"

"I want more," I said shamelessly. "I *need* more."

Malik definitely heard that, because the next thing I knew my legs were being lifted up into the air. I cried out as he made me spread my limbs open so wide I thought I would break. My head pressed into the pillows, and all I could feel was his powerful thrusts going downward into me, gravity helping him slide his massive, amazing dong even deeper into my depths. My body didn't belong to me at all. It was his and Allie's. And they could do whatever they wanted to it.

And just like that, without warning, shockwaves of pleasure violently ripped through me. My liquids began spilling out of me with the ferocity of a waterfall. It spattered everywhere—or that's what it felt like. I had been fucked in the ass until I'd cum. And Malik was still fucking me, even as I shook and shuddered and gasped through the orgasm. I knew no one cared that I'd cum. No one in the room cared about my pleasure. All they wanted was to take from me.

Malik let me fall to the bed and onto my own foul puddle of cum. Then he pulled me by the hair again and slapped me.

I whimpered as he towered over me, his hot breath warming my neck. "You like this, butters?" he thundered.

I bit my lip and nodded.

I could tell he was getting close. He was fucking me like an animal in heat. Every bone in my body ached.

Fuck. I wanted this to happen every day.

The torment had lasted for so long but I knew that when it was all over I'd think it ended too soon. My skin grated against the cuffs and Malik's cock slipped out. His hands stretched my crack open again, his thick fingers hooking themselves inside my asshole as he forced my body to open. His dripping cock bolted its way inside my asshole. I moaned. My little clit was hard all over again.

"Where would you like Malik to cum, babe?" Allie asked happily. She was trying to fix my hair. "Just a warning…he cums a *loooot.* Maybe I'll have him shoot it up your ass. Do you want to feel Malik explode inside your boipussy? Like he did in mine? God it feels amazing, especially in your ass. There's no feeling like that in the world." We made eye contact, and the fire in her face made me melt. "Do you want Malik to cum on your face? Ruin those pretty red lips? Your eyes? How about inside your mouth? Do you want to taste his cum?" She giggled. "Hmmm. I'll tell you what. How about we let Malik decide? You'll do whatever Malik wants, right?"

"I'll ruin that fucking mouth of hers," Malik said.

"Wow. That sounds perfect," Allie said before turning to me. "I know you're too tired to speak now so nod if you understand. I'll uncuff one arm so you can turn around and face both of us, okay?"

I nodded weakly.

The walls closed in as my wife unlocked the cuff off one wrist. The next thing I knew, Malik was pushing his throbbing penis into my mouth. His cum entered my throat like the rush of a raging river. Its hot, sour taste filled my mouth. Malik spurted some more, shooting load after load of his pleasure into me. Allie was shouting at me to take it all in. When my mouth was full I swallowed it all. She didn't know I'd had zero intention of spitting.

Once I sucked every drop of cum out of Malik and licked his manhood to perfection, Allie pulled me close and kissed me. It was the first kiss in a long time where I felt like she actually loved me. She smelled like Malik, but then again, I probably smelled like him too. It would've been impossible not to smell like that after having sex with a big man like him. My asshole was still shivering and puckering. Allie's tongue found mine and we both moaned. I thought about the flowers I'd bought her, still lying on the table. Hopefully a divorce wasn't in the cards any time soon.

I felt so full. And it wasn't just because of all the cum inside me. As Allie kept her lips on mine, I wondered how I could break it to her that I'd do anything to have this happen to me again. Have her dress me up like a slut and have her lover take me.

Maybe he could cum right in my ass next time. Allie would like that...

THE END

SISSIES IN HEAT
BLIND DATE

BLIND DATE

CHAPTER 1

"MITCH, YOUR PHONE'S BLOWING UP."

Vicky, my best friend, grabbed my phone off the balcony bar table and tossed it at me, but not before sneaking a peek at the screen.

I sighed as soon as I glanced at the phone. It was a slew of messages from Sabrina. We'd matched up six weeks ago and had met up for a beer before heading back to my place to hook up. Sabrina was a pretty blonde who was even prettier naked, but she was clingy as hell and wouldn't stop texting me after our one date.

Vicky saw me swipe up to ignore the notifications and her eyebrow shot up. She snatched my phone and began looking through my message trail.

"Dude. She's gorgeous," she said after a while. "What the hell is wrong with you?"

I didn't feel like explaining the whole story so I just shrugged.

"I don't know," I said. I had a hunch that my penthouse had something to do with the fact that this otherwise normal, self-respecting college student was prepared to beg—increasingly late into the night—for another date with me. I'd almost seen the dollar signs flashing in her pretty blue eyes when I'd showed her around that night.

"This is so not like you," Vicky said. "Are you okay? What happened to the sex-crazed Mitch I knew a year ago?"

"He's still in here," I insisted.

I looked over at the forest of condo buildings and the stretch of gray lake beyond, all casted in the orange glow of the sunset, and suddenly, the worst feeling in the world settled over me like a dark veil. My heart sank when I realized what it was. *Boredom.*

I was only twenty-seven. Life was still supposed to be exciting, wasn't it?

"I think I'm kind of in a rut," I finally admitted.

It felt marginally good to let it all out. Maybe the truth was that I'd been in a huge rut for a long time. Fucking just wasn't as fun anymore. My dates went all the same way: meet up at a bar near my place and assess our chemistry. If I got positive signals I'd take them back home and sooner or later we'd get down and dirty. My penthouse kind of worked like a magic trick— it was the surprise at the end that told my dates that I was a step above all the other men (nothing can get a girl to undress for you faster than exceeding their expectations). At first, having a new girl bare their body and soul to me was nothing short of a big sexual high. But now? I'd come to the realization that all my dates were basically all the same—same long hair...the same style of clothes...they even had the same long, drawn-out moan as they climaxed in my arms!

I glanced over at Vicky. She'd lapsed into silence after my confession, just sipping her Diet Coke. She was thinking.

We watched the sunset together.

"I have a great idea," she said after a minute or so. "You should go celibate for a year."

"That is an amazing idea," I said, downing my third beer—or was it my fourth? "Maybe you could tell me where I could get myself a monk's robe and shave my head too?"

Vicky laughed and crossed her legs. "When was the last time you had sex?"

I flinched and set my back against the wicker couch. "I wish I could ask you the same question."

Vicky thumped me on the arm. While she started going on her inevitable tirade, I tried to scan my memories. Forget about sex— when was the last time I'd had any *good* sex? The last time I'd fucked someone was maybe three weeks ago. But that was a sympathy fuck with a distant friend who'd just split up from her boyfriend, so that didn't count. Reeling back, all I could recollect was mindless, dumb, boring sex. I couldn't remember the last time I'd felt...what was the right word? *Taken...enthralled...swayed...*by a girl.

When I turned my attention back to Vicky, she was waving her arms around at the living room behind the balcony glass door. "And maybe, just maybe, Mitch, *this*—" Her waving became more frantic. "*This* is the problem. It's become sort of a...crutch, I think."

"Are you kidding me?" I asked. "I'm not giving up what I worked so hard for."

"You mean what your *dad* worked so hard for?" she bit back. *Ouch.*

"I have another great idea," Vicky continued brightly.

"Let me guess," I said. "Stay celibate for *two* years."

"No, idiot. I'm going to set you up."

"Oh yeah? With who?"

"Cherry."

The first thing I imagined was a stripper. "Who's that? A stripper?"

"Not a stripper. She's a friend. She's a little…different."

"No thanks."

Vicky was a self-confessed sapiosexual who loved rubbing in the fact she valued intelligence and personality more than looks. I was fine with that, but 'different' for Vicky could very well mean 'ugly', and I wasn't prepared to take the risk.

Vicky sighed. "And to think I thought you were starting to get a little more open-minded."

"I am," I shot back. "I just have no motivation to date a five-head you know?"

Vicky crumpled up her can of Diet Coke and aimed it at the trash can set at the corner of my wraparound balcony. She missed. She stood up and started ambling toward the can, grumbling.

"What if I told you Cherry's hot?"

I was back to watching the sunset when Vicky's proclamation reached my ears. I turned toward her. "Well, that definitely changes things."

She looked at me a little curiously. "When was the last time you cut your hair?"

I ran a hand through my hair. My last cut had been three months ago and had cost me $300. I'd kind of been digging the long look. "Dude. Should I start calling you Mom now?"

Vicky smiled. "I'll let you know when the date's all set up!"

"Hold on," I said. "I haven't exactly agreed to this great big date yet."

"Oh, but you will!" she said. "I can see that. You're intrigued, aren't you?"

"Well, you did tell me she's hot. So what makes her different?"

Vicky smiled mischievously. "I guess you'll find out."

The conversation that evening was left at that. We went out for a movie after, and oddly enough, I found myself thinking about Cherry. I hadn't even *thought* about a girl for a long time, and what was funny was I didn't even know what she looked like. For all I knew she could turn up with wonky teeth and crossed eyes—this was Vicky's version of 'hot' we were talking about after all. Maybe Cherry had a prosthetic leg or something…something I wouldn't exactly be opposed to. Still, I wasn't going to get my hopes up.

CHAPTER 2

THREE DAYS LATER, I'D ALL BUT forgotten about Cherry. I was at the gym focusing on my squats when Vicky called me up and said that I was supposed to meet up with Cherry at her place the next day.

I was more than a little thrown off by the suggestion.

"At her place?" I asked hesitantly. "What if she turns out to be a...I don't know, a serial killer?"

Vicky just sighed dramatically into my ear.

"Alright, alright," I said. "I get it." All Vicky was doing was gently nudging me out of my comfort zone. As best friends do. I wasn't exactly opposed to meeting Cherry at her place. Didn't that make things easier? I could skip all the small talk and bullshit. Of course, that meant I couldn't rely on my penthouse to add to my sex appeal. That was okay. I was still funny, smart, and sexy.

This was definitely going to be a little different.

"She'll be making dinner," Vicky added.

"Awesome."

"I'll text you the address."

As soon as she hung up I keyed the place into Google Maps and frowned. Cherry's place was a little more than an hour and a half away. She wasn't exactly a 'city' girl.

The next evening, I got home early from work and started getting ready for my big blind date. A fresh white linen shirt, my favorite Balmain jeans, my suede Tom Ford loafers. A splash of cologne. A dash of Moroccan oil through my hair. Plenty of anti-perspirant. I took a whiff of my shirt to make sure the guy at the laundromat hadn't used one of those awful scent boosters. Nope. Just nice, clean fabric.

All the time I'd gained from leaving work early was lost on my way to Cherry's place. I'd entered the wrong address into the GPS which sent me ten miles eastward before I'd noticed the mistake. By the time I reached Cherry's house, it was a half-hour past our agreed-upon time, which was 8 p.m.

Cherry's house was located in a fairly isolated community, encircled by luscious greenery and thick, brushy woods. It was obvious this wasn't just any community. I drove past the open gates and parked out front, then skipped up the pathway leading up to the front entrance. I wondered if she lived alone.

There's no way she's living in that giant house all alone, I thought, rolling my eyes. I just hoped the 'rents were out for the night.

When the door opened, my mouth suddenly went dry and my breathing got a little heavier.

Cherry was a drop dead gorgeous redhead.

She was wearing this pretty red dress that matched seamlessly with her hair, which reached down to her waist. She also had a hair clip that kind of bunched up one side of her hair and let it fall strategically off her face. The top of her dress showed off the nice round shape of a set of very perky tits.

"Hi," she said. "You must be Mitchell."

"Uh, Mitch," I said, and cracked a smile. "Sorry I'm late."

I couldn't help but notice that her eyes were so light they might as well have been made of glass.

She shrugged lightly. "Please, come in."

I was instantly blown away by the interior of the house. Decorated by neutrals and subtle accent colors, everything screamed excess wealth. The floors almost sparkled and the huge wall paintings showed off shapes and patterns that were modern in the way they didn't really make any sense. In the living room, expensive textures like pure silk and cashmere adorned most of the throws and pillows decorating the furniture. And—*of course*— there was a grand piano.

Cherry invited me to sit on this huge leather couch positioned in front of an expansive wall art made of cracked china plates. I settled my feet on top of the ornate rug that spanned the floor and tried not to get lost in its elaborate swirls. Cherry pressed a button on the side of the wall and a TV began sliding down inconspicuously from the ceiling, already playing some kind of news channel. Then she went to fix me a drink, telling me she'd be right back.

I took the opportunity to text Vicky a quick: '*Your eyes still work after all*'. I couldn't read the catty reply back because Cherry returned with two drinks balanced on a tray.

I'd already thought of the perfect ice-breaker. "So, how do you know Vicky?"

"We go way back," she said, not caring to offer any further specifics. She flopped down on the couch opposite mine and brought her knees up, hugging her drink and getting comfortable. "I wasn't expecting you to be this handsome."

I gave her a smirk, trying not to give anything else away from my expression.

I didn't expect you to be this hot. Or this wealthy. What the heck does your family do?

"Do you live with your parents?" I asked.

"Oh no," Cherry said. "My parents actually live in London. With my brother, Casey. They come visit me every six months or so."

My ear perked up. Vicky had been to London. On some kind of exchange student scholarship program.

"London? Then what are you doing *here*?"

"I grew up there," she admitted. "Well, half here, and half in England I guess. My mom works for the United Nations, and my dad's British so we never stayed in one place for too long." She blew adorably at a stray strand of hair that had fallen across her face. "As for why I'm still here, I'm not sure, I guess I just feel more at home. And London weather can get pretty rubbish. I get depressed whenever I visit."

"That's cool," I said. "You don't have an accent or anything."

"Oh, that's because I do a lot of code-switching," Cherry said, giving me another one of her light shrugs. "Need a refill?" she asked, pointing to my now empty glass.

"Sure," I said.

When she disappeared from my line of vision, I settled back on the couch and brought my legs up, daring to get a little messy in her spotless space. *Hot, rich, and nice,* I thought. *So what's the catch?* Vicky had said she was *different*. Different how? Unless she'd been talking about the fact that Cherry was rolling in money, I didn't exactly smell that anything was off.

CHAPTER 3

CHERRY AND I SPENT ANOTHER HOUR or so chit-chatting in her living room. The topics never veered away from first date vibes: movies (Cherry's dad had an extensive DVD collection which we went through), hobbies (she loved running, pilates, and reading), and books (her favorite author? Richard Matheson). When I asked her what she did, Cherry was surprisingly evasive.

"I'm not doing anything too ambitious right now," she said. "I write, but mostly just for myself."

I took that as code for: *I can afford to do anything I fucking want.*

Which…I could kind of relate to. Kind of.

The whole time, I was trying to urge myself to make a move. If this was like any of my other dates, we'd both be naked right now and things would've been so intense she'd witness an entire galaxy of stars just from my cock screwing her tight, pink pussy. Today, though…all I could do was watch her from the couch, noticing the soft freckles across her nose and the perfect angles that made up her face. There was something about Cherry that was making me really, really like her.

"You know, you don't need to sit that far out," she said suddenly. "There's plenty of space here." She extended a foot onto the side of her couch.

I grinned. "I was waiting until you asked."

Cherry placed her legs on my lap as soon as I settled in.

She has pretty feet, I thought. I'd never been into feet, but I couldn't help but think hers were flawless. They were small, perfectly polished with some dark glitter, and looked so delicate. I had the sudden urge to bite down on her big toe, to taste her softness...

Cherry caught me staring down at her feet. My cheeks instantly felt as hot as an oven.

Was I blushing? Jesus Christ!

"So you never told me how you know Vicky," I said, trying to break the awkward silence.

"I don't think we're here to talk about her," she chided me gently. "Are you hungry?"

The fact that she'd brushed me off so easily settled on me uneasily while we headed to the dining room. I suddenly wished we were at my place instead, curled up in my bed or doing it on top of the kitchen island. Without my old routine to set me on track, I had to be on my toes and I didn't exactly like it.

"Wow," I said when I took a bite out of the steaming stew. "Did you make this yourself?"

"Uh-huh," Cherry said.

"What's in there?"

"Rabbit. And like four different types of mushrooms."

We ate, and at that point it got a little awkward. Which wasn't a good sign. It wasn't a good sign at all. You wanted a date to get warmer and hotter by the second, not cooler. I knew I'd have to do double duty now if I wanted the night to end well.

"Wanna go to the garden?" Cherry said once we were done with dessert. "It's pretty nice out there at this time."

A backyard garden at night was a great place to make a move. Chicks liked flowers and romantic starry skies, didn't they? I could easily woo her there.

It turned out that Cherry had wanted to give me a whole backyard tour. I made it a point to stand close to her, brushing her arm casually as I wished I could shut her mouth up once and for all by thrusting my cock inside those pretty lips. The thought led me to have a full-blown erection.

Yes. Rip that red dress off, Mitch, and eat her ass under the stars. See how she'd like it.

"I wanna show you something," Cherry said suddenly.

Before I could react, she'd taken my hand and was pulling me through to a shed that was in the corner of her backyard. Our footwear plunged into the muddy trail that led to it—a black corrugated shed that seemed like it could've functioned as an out office except for the fact that there were no windows. The dinner that I'd just had was now bubbling away in my stomach, and I tried to let out a burp as quietly as I could.

Cherry opened the door with a skull key that was hidden under a flower pot by the side of the shed. She whooshed me inside before flicking on the lights. The room lit up hazily, like there was just candlelight. I saw blood-red and black, along with shadows and more darkness. A constrained space that nevertheless seemed to hold an endless array of things.

I wasn't sure what I'd expected, but it definitely wasn't *this*.

I'd imagined a studio or an artist's space or something…but this…this was a BDSM room.

A *dungeon.*

I was at a loss for words as I took it all in. Cherry's 'shed' was equipped with everything you could possibly think of. There was a life-size cross to one side, its silver cuffs falling seductively off each end. Dildos and whips and weird-looking gadgets were propped up on low shelves. An umbrella holder held a dizzying array of canes of different lengths and colors. There was an entire *bed* along the other side. It was a gothic-style four-poster bed accompanied by a small red velvet chair and a footstool.

"What do you think?" Cherry asked.

You are one kinky bitch.

"Looks painful," I joked, grinning. This was perfect. So *this* was why Vicky had said that Cherry was different. She just had eclectic tastes. Whatever. It was hot. All my worries about the night ending in disaster disappeared into the night. I imagined cuffing her to that giant cross, peppering those round tits of hers with kisses while she had to endure my endless teasing to her clit. My boner sprang back to life.

Cherry seemed blissfully unaware of my dark thoughts. She sat down on the bed like an angel and ran a hand through her gorgeous red hair. She knew exactly what she was doing and I was drinking it all up. I saw her give me a little smile and I smirked. Right then, funnily enough, I couldn't give a fuck about her playroom. I just wanted to bang her.

I went close to her and started playing with her hair. She smelled like an impending night-long fuck-fest. Her body seemed to want to stick to mine. Before we knew it, we were making out.

I breathed hard into her and crept one hand inside her dress, rubbing the soft apex atop her thighs. It was already damp. Craving something. *Me.*

I sucked in a breath and yanked her legs far apart, burying my hands inside to get rid of her panties.

Cherry stopped me.

"I'd like to try something with you," she said brightly.

The candlelight illuminating her light eyes and freckles was making her look even more stunning. I stared into those eyes before I nodded. We were in her dungeon, after all. I wasn't opposed to trying something new.

She made me lay down on the bed. I was expecting feathers and cushiony goodness, but the 'bed' was hard. It wasn't *really* a bed, I realized. Just a structure made up to kind of imitate one.

Then out of nowhere, Cherry basically jumped my bones.

"Whoa!" I huffed out as her entire weight descended on me.

Her tongue was inside my mouth as she unbuttoned my shirt. The shed felt hot and cool at the same time, and I thought there was a breeze coming from outside. But as she went on to attack my jeans, I saw that the door was firmly shut and the breeze was being created by a small rotating fan attached close to the ceiling. We were literally shut off from the world in this tiny space that was catered to Cherry's fantasies.

The next second, my boxers were on the floor and I was stark naked. My cock was being enthusiastically spat on and then Cherry was jerking me off.

"Are you like a Mistress or something?" I couldn't help but ask.

Cherry straddled my legs and laughed. "Nah. Like I said, I'm a writer. I like writing erotic stories. It's a little bit of an alternate profession, so I mostly like to keep it to myself."

She tightened her grip on my shaft and I choked out a moan. I stretched my arms behind my head and got comfy—or as much as I could on the hard bed so I could relax into this handjob. Cherry was good at this. *Great.* I suddenly remembered that she'd wanted to try something different. What it was…I still didn't know.

"Tell me when you're close," she said in this husky voice. "Really close."

She was still pumping me. Slowly now. Strategically. I was getting real sensitive, my dick veins throbbing with mounting lust. I was probably three inches away from the wetlands of her pussy. She amped up her pace. I marveled at how shiny my cock looked with her hot spit.

"I'm close," I breathed.

Instead of upping the pace, Cherry completely let go. My cock jerked up and I felt my body vibrate with hunger only to then fizz out in disappointment. I gritted my teeth.

Your idea of different is giving me blue balls?

Cherry laughed heartily when she saw my expression. I was mildly annoyed but she clearly gave no fucks. I guess it was hard to give a fuck when you were buck naked while your date was still fully dressed with not a hair out of place. She knew exactly what she was doing.

With that hot smug look still on her face, she leaned back on her elbows and spread her legs. Her dress rode up her thighs and the strip of her underwear greeted me, gray and shadowy, but presumably black in reality. Her weight was on my still pulsing cock. I wished I had taken off her panties earlier.

"Aw. Come on now. Let's put a smile back on that handsome face," she teased.

I gritted my teeth harder. I hated all the teasing but I also kind of loved it. Normally I was the one doing all the teasing. The taunting. A girl had to *really* like you if she was doing it. It was just making me want to fuck her harder when the time came.

She brought her legs down, resting them on each of my shoulders. Her heels sank into my flesh.

"I didn't know you had a foot fetish," she said. She was grinding against my fresh boner.

I didn't say a single word.

"Still okay with trying something different?"

"Heck yeah," I said.

Even her stupid fan couldn't cool me down now.

She teased me with those heels again, brushing the tips against the side of my cheeks. The bottoms were caked with mud and silt, and they definitely smelled that way. I was sweating. I couldn't put a finger on why what she was doing was so fucking *sensual*. The way she lay confidently on top of me, her legs spread, like my body was her only source of comfort in her hospital bed. Those sharp heels pressing hard into my shoulder blades. Promising me just a touch of danger.

One muddy sole nudged against my cheek.

"Lick it," she whispered.

CHAPTER 4

I STARED AT CHERRY, WHO HAD HER eyebrow raised like she was taunting me. I stared down at the dirty black heel cradled against my cheek and right shoulder. Then I shut my eyes.

She said something that made my dick squirm with wanting.

"If you do it right I might just take off my panties for you."

I leaned further into the heel, the strong odor of muck surrounding me. It was a pretty dirty thing to do—literally—but I knew I was going to do it. I grinned at Cherry as I grasped the sole with my tongue, bringing the muddy surface to my lips. The actual heel part—which looked to be about five inches tall—was literally *caked* with mud. Cherry was staring down at me intensely as I licked, tentatively as first, and then with a little more gusto. Her foot stayed still, letting me explore the depths of her designer heel. The air was positively pregnant with tension.

"You're such a bootlicker," she murmured. She began wiping her heel against my tongue, urging me to clean it faster.

Dirty, dirty. I rolled my mouth against the sole, trying to ignore the incredible saltiness of the mud cake I was tasting. I was doing this for *her*.

"I think I'm going to need a little motivation here," I said after a while, my eyes darting between her legs.

Cherry tittered. "And *I* think you can do a little better. Open your mouth."

The moment I did, she popped her five-inch heel inside like it was nothing.

"Can you suck it?" she asked.

I was technically already sucking it, because she was jutting it in and out like it was a cock in *her* mouth. I was swallowing mud now, and a little thrill whiffed down my spine as the odor of her foot finally reached me. Okay, maybe I definitely had a foot fetish, and I wasn't totally upset. There was just something so dirty sexual about what I was doing, polishing her soiled footwear off, sucking it off just to please her.

As the smell of her foot lingered I was getting more and more aroused. Cherry seemed satisfied with how clean her high heel was because she popped it out through my lips before thrusting the left one in. By now, the sucking motions were becoming automatic…my head bobs and her heel pumping in perfect synchrony…all I could imagine was her hot pussy slobbering over me next while I sucked off that delicious clit of hers…

"Ugh, a submissive guy is *such* a turn on," Cherry breathed. She snuck her heel out, laughing when she saw that my mouth was still in an 'O' position. "Okay. I think it's time for your reward."

Not breaking eye contact, Cherry got rid of her black underwear. She leaned forward and, with zero warning, rubbed her panties on my face.

"Oh fuck—" I mumbled, inhaling her scent, letting it soak down to my bones.

"Shhhh…" she whispered. I could smell her breath this time. "Dragonfruit."

"Dragonfruit?"

"That's your safeword. If you feel like things are getting too fucked up. Or if you want to take a break. Anyway. Remember the word."

"Got it, Mistress."

Fucked up? I almost wanted to chuckle. Just how fucked up could things get, now that'd licked and swallowed the mud off her feet?

She was now at the back of the bed, on her knees, twirling her underwear like a cowboy's lasso while staring at me seductively. A playful grin spread on her face and she hunched down to thrust the two panty holes up my legs.

"What are you—" I grunted.

But things were happening too fast for me to even process them. When I looked down I was no longer naked. I was wearing her panties.

"How does it feel? Too tight?" Cherry asked.

I was too focused on the feel of the fabric to answer her right away. The crotch was definitely *wet*. Her pussy juice-drenched panties were clinging onto my balls, making me want to groan with need.

"It's…it's okay," I bit out after a while.

"Remember the safeword?"

I nodded.

"Good." Cherry got back to work. She peeled her dress off

and unstrapped her bra. My heart was beating like a horse in a race at the sight of her naked body. The fact she was revealing herself to me after such a long wait was making me happy, but at the same time she was—very purposefully—dressing me up in *her* clothes. There was a sense of pride in what she was doing. Quick, stern, deliberate motions. Like I was a shiny but lifeless doll she'd just bought from the toy store.

"Has anyone said you'd make a good woman?" she whispered.

"Not really," I said breathlessly.

"Well, you are," she said. "You don't even need a wig." Her fingers tousled my hair a little, and then she took off her hair clip and clipped it on mine. "Hold on."

From somewhere she's taken out a tube of lipgloss. She applied a layer onto her lips, rubbing them to allow the shine to settle before smearing some onto mine very slowly, like she wanted to milk every ounce of enjoyment she was getting out of it.

"You're very pretty, Mitchy," she said and planted a glossy peck on my cheek.

She pulled away but then she came back to me. She kissed me like I was irresistible. This time, we were soft and gentle, our tongues kissing in slow motion. I grabbed her naked breast and squeezed it, content to tickle her nipple until it hardened underneath my fingers. She responded by squeezing *mine*. Pressing and pinching my nipple through the bra cup. I could feel it shoot up and swell underneath the dress. We were acting like a lesbian couple or something, and I was so confused. What the heck was my blind date doing to me?

When Cherry finally broke away my dick had its own

heartbeat. She reached underneath the pillow and pulled out something that sparkled under the dim lights. It was a tiara. She raked it through my hair and it easily gripped itself into place.

"I only do this for special dates," she said.

I blushed. I suddenly felt like a shy teenage girl, and it was *so wrong*. But I was special, apparently. And my dick liked it.

Cherry was incredibly good at reading my thoughts. "It's meant to be weird and confusing," she said in this matronly tone, like she was guiding me through an awkward coming-of-age experience. "That's okay. As long as you still like it. You do, don't you?"

I found myself nodding. This was all kinds of fucked up but I was too shy to admit that I weirdly liked it out loud.

Cherry looked delighted. "Wow. I'm glad you like it, Mitchy," she said. "You look hot in red and that tiara looks so cute on you. And I love that you're wearing my tiny little girlie panties. You make me so *wet*."

She was now leaning against a small wooden cabinet, letting me enjoy her perfect silhouette. Her orange pubic hair was trimmed but not shaped in any kind of way, and I was loving how it curled outward unashamedly. Each curl glistened with evidence of her lust.

She opened the cabinet and pulled out a coil of black rope, thick as a snake.

I struggled to take in a breath. She was going to tie me up. Wasn't she? She had made me into a woman and now she was going to bind me up. *And do what?* I realized I was sweating profusely, and my armpits felt slick and slimy.

Why the fuck was I so nervous? *Cherry* made me nervous. She was so unpredictable.

CHAPTER 5

OF COURSE, MY INTUITION HAD BEEN RIGHT.

My wrists were tied up first, my arms brought up and behind my head. Cherry started wrapping the rope around me like I was someone's Christmas present, criss-crossing it over my chest in an elaborate pattern. I was breathing heavily, sweating, and feeling light-headed and strangely helpless—claustrophobic in my own body. But the feeling passed just as quickly as it had descended over me. It was such a paradox, but Cherry was strangely caring in the way she was tying me up. Full of pride like before, paying attention to the knots she was making so they didn't hurt me.

"Oh, Cherry…" I wheezed. I was so breathless. *So horny.*

Cherry smiled cryptically.

No more words were exchanged.

She was building up the knots on my chest. Once she was done she brought my knees up and off the bed, binding my thighs to my shins, connecting the ties to the knots on my chest.

It was when she giggled and yanked at my cock like it was a hidden treasure that I realized she'd essentially frozen my body in missionary position. I couldn't move my legs and my knees were tied up to my chest, my legs spread wide. Giving her free access to my pantied crotch.

Cherry straddled me, sinking her body between my legs.

"You look so much like Ian right now," she murmured.

"Ian?" I mumbled. "Vicky's ex?"

Cherry nodded.

None of what she was saying was making sense. "What do you mean?" I asked.

She began hugging me tight, pressing her pillowy tits down onto my stomach. "So. I first met Vicky in Chelsea, and like three years later our paths crossed at a sex party. She was into BDSM at the time." She laughed at my incredulous face. I had no idea Vicky was anywhere close to the BDSM scene at *any* point in time. "The party was wild. We did a makeover on Ian, made him wear a wig and a dress, and tied him up just like you. It was so hot. And then…you want to know what we did to him?" She trailed her fingers down my chest and into my non-existent cleavage. I'd already stopped breathing right then. "We took turns fucking him. Oh yes, Mitchy. Don't look so surprised. It was Vicky's idea at first but when she was actually doing it I could see she wasn't all that into it…but me? I'd always wanted to fuck a guy. And oh my god, it's like the best feeling in the world. You should've heard Ian moaning and crying. I think he enjoyed it more than I did, and *that's* saying something!"

Cherry was now grinding against my ass. It was impossible not to get aroused with her dancing against my cock and I was struggling against my own urges. *This isn't how things were supposed to go.* I was supposed to be the charmer. The seductor. The *man.* All of my old habits and routines were seeping out of me and they were being replaced by something new and dangerous.

"Oh god! Oh god!" I suddenly screamed.

Cherry was tickling me. Her laughter echoed inside the shed, getting increasingly warped and sinister as I writhed helplessly against the thick ropes enveloping my body. I felt so vulnerable, tears dripping down my face as she ruthlessly tickled my underarms and neck. She could really do anything she wanted to me right now, and here I was in a prime position with my legs and ass out just for her.

I just had to watch and wait to see what she'd do to me next...

"Still okay?" she whispered as the tickling died down.

"Yeah," I muttered. My eyes stung and there was a gigantic lump in my throat. The fact that she was checking in on me was so fucking hot. It was weirdly romantic too. All this was making me feel so *wrong*, like I was a girl who was about to lose her virginity.

"Don't you want to gag me?" I teased when I found my voice again.

Cherry shook her head. "I'm not the biggest fan of gags. Like, I want to talk to you while I do it. Hear you moan...hear you beg. That's what really turns me on, you know? Why? Do you want me to gag you?"

"No. I...I think I'm interested in doing this the way you want to," I replied.

"Perfect." Cherry lovingly removed her heels and squeezed my feet into them. "*You're* perfect."

"No, you," I joked, even though it felt like the furthest thing from a joke.

Cherry towered over my face and slowly began humping me.

Her long hair fell over my face as we both started feeling good together, me shadowing her motions as I had no choice but to rock along with her. I almost wanted to chuckle about how disastrously my date night had gone. To think that I'd finally met a girl who didn't bore me to death only to find out she wanted to seduce and feminize me. Wrap me around her hot little pussy and suck her high heels just because she told me so. I thought of Vicky and suddenly felt embarrassed. There was no doubt my best friend knew what Cherry would try on me tonight.

Oh god. There was no way I could face Vicky again.

"Holy shit, Mitchy," Cherry moaned into my ear. "I'm so wet. I don't think I can wait a second longer. I need to make you my sissy bitch."

She got up from the bed and walked back toward the shadows off the far end of the shed, where I heard her opening another one of her cabinets. Several objects rattled around as she searched in the dark for what she wanted. When she sauntered back to where I was, something long and regal was curving out from between her hips.

A cock.

Cherry's tits bounced violently as she hopped onto the bed and towered over me again. I was breathless again, the lump returning to my throat. The hot pink apparatus almost glowed in the shadows. I swallowed thickly, wishing I could wipe away the river of sweat that was now flowing down my back. How could a chick with a pink silicone penis look so hot?

"Do you like my cock?" Cherry asked me sultrily.

"Uh…it's pretty big," I squeaked. Her penis was now digging into my groin and making me shiver.

She smiled. "Scared?"

"A little," I admitted.

"Well, you know what to do." Her smile widened. "I adore you, Mitchy."

"I adore you too," I whispered.

Who the fuck had I become, spewing sappy shit out of my mouth?

We both nodded at each other and laughed together. Her feminine warmth felt amazing to me. My nerves melted and I felt safe with her, even though we were about to do something incredibly, disgustingly taboo.

She scooted up my body and flapped her cock on my lips. "Suck it," she murmured, her glassy eyes shining with excitement. "Suck it like a good girl."

CHAPTER 6

I BLINKED UP AT CHERRY. I'D JUST been hit by a wave of déjà vu because that had been eerily close to how *I* did it with women. The flap and the thrust. *Suck it, slut. You know you want to.* That was what I might've said to Cherry on another night.

Without thinking, I bent forward and wrapped my lips around the tip of the cock. As I began to suck, a wave of revulsion rushed over me. This was worse than licking off those muddy, dirty heels. The soft, spongy feel on my tongue was tricking me into thinking this was a real penis. Cherry ordered me to put my tongue out and then she held onto the railings as she began to fuck my mouth. I groaned as the dildo sank into my open jaw again and again and again. As disgusted as I was, I was still hard—unimaginably, shamelessly hard—and I was leaking into Cherry's panties.

The abuse of my mouth stopped only once Cherry was satisfied. She gave me a soft peck on my cheek and lifted herself off of me, leaving me to suck in the drool that was still oozing out of my lips. Her head disappeared between my thighs and I gasped as her cold teeth nipped at my skin. She tore away my panties like a tigress in heat, spitting out shreds of fabric onto the bedspread.

I felt faint.

Good god, that was so hot.

Wasn't it just mere minutes ago that I was fantasizing about how hard I'd fuck Cherry? Desperate to give her the pounding she deserved? Was I even that same Mitch? It was like every single trace of manhood left inside me was dying. A part of me was nervous if I'd even wake up as Mitch tomorrow. Maybe I'd stay girly forever…begging hot girls to fuck me in the butt for the rest of my damned life…

"We'll take it easy," Cherry was saying gently, wiping away some of the sweat from my inner thighs. "Since you're technically a virgin tonight. But I promise you it's going to feel really good soon." She winked at me, and my heart stopped. "I can't wait to hear you moaning, Mitchy."

I licked my lips and winked back, even though I doubted that would happen. I wasn't like Ian. Vicky's ex-boyfriend was tall, intelligent, but he was also—in the nicest way possible—rather effeminate. He took longer than Vicky to get ready and always talked about what a dream it would be to get into fashion school. Ian might've moaned like a girl while he was tied up and getting blasted in the ass and he might've really wanted it, but I was different. I just thought it was hot that a naked girl with a strap-on was going to fuck me while I pretended to be a girl, but even though I'd embraced the whole crossdressing thing today, there was simply no way my ass could override years of cock juicing.

Cherry rubbed the lining of my asshole for a minute or so,

warming it up before her index finger—drenched with saliva—glided inside me. I was taking it like a champ. There was no way I could describe how that first time felt, except when she thrust her middle finger in, my asshole was full and hot and pulsing. My thighs strained against the rope, and my left leg had already fallen asleep. I wriggled my toes inside my heels, bracing when my leg prickled as it woke up.

When she lined her pink cock against my puckered hole, I almost wanted to shut my eyes. Did I really want to see this? I was horny now, and I decided I did. I didn't want to miss the moment Cherry took my virginity.

I let out a hiss as her thick cock head penetrated me. *Breathe.* I curved my spine a little, hoping it would make it easier for it to further intrude into my depths. *Breathe.* The feeling of humiliation was so overwhelming now that I was leaking. Precum seeped onto my stomach as she coerced her bulky toy into my impossibly tight asshole. True to her promise, Cherry was being very gentle, almost motherly, trying not to hurt me. Even though she could've completely obliterated my anus if she'd wanted to.

"Shhh. Shhh…" she said, massaging my upper thigh. "You're okay. You're doing great. I'm here…we're so close. So close."

Her massage was really grounding me, and I realized I'd been hyperventilating.

Not nearly as macho as you thought, huh, Mitch?

"Fuck, Mitchy, you're way tighter than I thought," Cherry said. The words lingered above us, sending chills through my heart. The bed rocked a little as she hunted for something underneath the mattress. I heard her pop something open, and cold lube was slathered and poked down my crack and through my asshole. Her cock head, now soppier and kinder to my virgin ass, penetrated me once more. Her lashes fluttered as she blinked down furiously, trying to concentrate on the task at hand. Full of wanting. Determined to still fuck me.

The cock was finally gliding in. I tried to clench and unclench my anus to help push it further along, as Cherry spread my shuddering ass cheeks apart. That was all I could do, wasn't it? Seconds later, she started pumping. I felt myself open up as we swayed together. I wasn't sure how many inches had gone inside me, but it certainly felt like a truckload.

I knew that we'd made progress when she loomed above me and we shared a kiss.

Our tongues slipped and slid against each other and her hot breath almost made me lose it. When we pulled apart she spat straight into my open mouth before she hunkered down again, caressing my lips like she never wanted to let go. Her spit was delicious. When I'd swallowed it all I opened my mouth again, inviting more of her mouth nectar. Cherry rewarded me with even more spit this time as a huge spurt spewed out from her mouth to mine. I made the gooey fluid swivel around in my mouth as we made out. The pull between us was as strong as a wildfire. She felt so powerful, so *masculine* as she fucked me, and I'd never felt smaller or more desired. Even though she was ignoring my cock, it was all starting to feel a little too good.

"Please, Cherry, please…fuck me harder." I was gasping now, exhaling the words like I'd lost my voice.

"Ask like a slut and maybe I'll do it," Cherry murmured, chewing her lip as she stared down at me so intensely I couldn't help but blush.

"Please, Cherry?" I begged in this cute, girly voice. "I would do anything for you to fuck me like you wanted to destroy me. I just need to feel your cock. Please."

"I think you can do even better, Mitchy."

I blushed harder, feeling the blood rush to my privates as I felt her heat. I closed my eyes as I begged, too shy to see her face.

"Look at what you've done to me, Cherry. I've become such a cock slut. My ass needs your cock to drill into me like my lungs need air." I stopped short, trying desperately to put my horny feelings into words. "I'm your sissy bitch and you know it. You know what I need now. I'm your bitch toy waiting to be used and abused."

At this point Cherry had stopped fucking me. Her eyes glazed over mine as she listened to my embarrassing pleas. Taunting me.

"More."

I felt my privates throb as the words tumbled out. "My tight virgin hoe ass needs to be fucked hard. I'd lick your muddy heels everyday for the rest of my life if you can bang my booty hard tonight. I need to feel the pain of you ripping my dirty, nasty little butthole apart with your amazing strong cock. I need you to hurt me. Please. Pretty please with a cherry on top!"

My breath was knocked out of me as she started fucking me again with a fury I hadn't seen before. Her hip thrusts felt euphoric and as I stared down at myself all I could see were my legs spread eagle and my heels shaking to her rhythm. I wrestled against my restraints, my wrists getting rubbed raw as my body squirmed in response to the pounding. But I didn't care. I was Cherry's hot little bitch and I didn't give a damn. I only wanted to be used.

"Take it, whore!" Cherry rasped. "You desperate, pathetic sissy slut!"

She grabbed handfuls of my ass cheeks, painfully spreading my crack wide open as rammed into me with the force of a million cocks hitting at once.

She was hitting the spot. *The* spot.

In an instant, all hell broke loose.

My balls tightened as my milk shot up high into the air. Pleasure thundered through my body like a hurricane that was sweeping my entire existence away. Tears sprung to my eyes as I tried to buck in response to my climax but failed, forced instead to stay still and power through the insane pulsing that was taking over my body.

"Holy shit," I whispered after what felt like an hour. "I think that was the most overwhelming orgasm I've ever had."

"Trust me, I can see that," Cherry said. She swiped my cum off my dress and held her finger to my lips. "Eat this for me."

I sucked her finger happily. I would've done anything for her at that moment.

Cherry finally untied me and I groaned and stretched freely, feeling the bliss of freedom. She got rid of the tiara, the heels, and my hair clip and fixed my hair, which was now a sweaty, stinky mess. Cherry didn't seem to mind. She spooned me from behind and we cooled down, *very* casually, like she hadn't just pounded the shit out of me seconds earlier.

"You know, Mitchy, you've been such a good girl I wouldn't be opposed to you spending the night," Cherry said minutes later.

"I'd love to," I said.

"What are you going to tell Vicky?" she asked, hugging me tight.

"I have no idea," I began. "I…I think I'll have no choice but to tell her the truth. She's good at squeezing the truth out of me anyway."

I couldn't help but blush again as I thought about how that conversation would go.

As I sank back into Cherry's warm body, my eyes flickered toward a small shelf of books that was directly across from me. I squinted to make out the title on the spine. *Seducing the Sissy,* by Cherry Blakey. I found myself grinning. So…she wasn't such an unknown writer after all. In any case, she'd definitely found a new fan.

THE END

SISSIES IN HEAT
FEMDOM MAID

FEMDOM MAID

CHAPTER 1

"PLEASE…YOU CAN'T TELL HER," I pleaded.

Our maid, Lena, barely looked up at me from the TV screen.

"You have sixty seconds, Mrs. Martin," she said, completely ignoring my plea. She tapped inattentively on her Apple watch, reminding me of the timer she'd set. The unsent message was on her phone, ready to go off to my wife as soon as time was up. *Claudia, I thought you deserved to know that Shane is a pervert.*

I shivered at the thought and proceeded to vigorously wipe the cleaner off the stove. I grabbed the old stack of magazines and flyers that had been building up by the fridge. It released a plume of dust straight into my nostrils.

"Lena…she might come home any second now," I wheezed.

The TV went mute. "Do I look like I care?" Lena asked, her voice flat and emotionless. "The more time you spend whining the sooner she'll find out."

The TV blared once again, louder this time. I sighed and got back to work, wiping the edge of the countertop. I wasn't supposed to speak. I was just supposed to be working. My short maid's skirt swished to and fro while I bent over the counters and moved steadily to get rid of grime and dirt. Once I was done with the right side I gave Lena a secret glance. *Dang.* If only she wasn't so hot. Lena had the sort of beauty that played tricks on you and made you make some very bad decisions. She was sprawled out on our couch with her legs up and her small pretty feet dangling off the edge. She had a headband in her curly blonde hair and the only makeup she had on seemed to be a little gloss on the lips. She was wearing a pair of denim overalls that were ripped at the knees and a white tank top underneath.

What kind of maid wears *white* to her cleaning gig? Oh, just Lena….because she wasn't actually doing any of the cleaning.

Less than two weeks ago, my wife hired Lena off one of our local Facebook groups. We had the money to spend, but more importantly, Claudia thought I was shitty at keeping house, though she didn't really say 'shitty' because she was nice like that. Claudia has always been the breadwinner with her job in tech sales, while I was a freelance writer—or that's what I liked to say to people. In truth, work had dried up and I was burnt out doing the cold-emailing and networking required to land myself a proper client. So the reality was more that I was a bum who lived off my hardworking wife.

Claudia decided that Lena would come over to clean for two hours every other day and four hours every weekend. She couldn't have known that hiring a hot college grad to practically live with me part-time would have…consequences.

On Lena's second day on the job I was feeling horny. *She* was making me horny. She always seemed to be braless and her nipples shamelessly poked through the thin tops she wore. That day, she was wearing a top that I could've sworn was just a silk handkerchief folded up front and tied up at the back. It barely contained her full Cs. To make matters worse, she was wearing these tiny shorts and was bent over vacuuming the big rug in our living room. I snuck behind the archway of the laundry room— our doorless laundry room connecting directly to the living space was just one of the quirks of our house—and estimated I could cum in less than two minutes if I started right that second, meaning I could finish with a good view of her ass before she was done with that rug.

I shouldn't have done it. I know that now. I was being an idiot, but that's what pretty girls like Lena do to you. They fuck up your thinking.

I had my hand on my cock and had boldly gravitated right smack in the middle of the archway when Lena abruptly turned around. I froze like a deer in headlights for only a millisecond. Then I started running, past the kitchen, up the stairs, past our home office and into our bedroom. I slammed the door behind me and collapsed on the floor, hiding my face in my hands.

That was how Lena found me. She just stared at me for a long time, watching me shaking, close to tears and on the verge of a panic attack. I wasn't the kind of person to take risks. I was—in all honesty—a softie. I was a nice guy, always polite, and especially polite to women. I *wasn't* the sort of guy who just brazenly dropped his pants and jerked off to the maid who was essentially working under me. If someone else had told me this story I would've said that it was a disgusting abuse of power.

In the long stretch of silence that day with me on the floor and Lena watching over me, I thought—maybe ridiculously—that she'd forgive me. But she didn't. She threatened to let my wife know what a pervert I was. And when I begged her that couldn't happen, she switched gears. The very next day, she brought me one of those sexy maid's costumes you'd wear to a Halloween party and a wig. Then she ordered me to start doing her job while she supervised me from the couch.

The moment I agreed to step into that maid's skirt and put on that wig, our roles were reversed. All her professionalism disappeared and she became a downright bitch to me.

My wife was now paying Lena a ridiculous amount of money just for me to do the housework…all over again.

While wiping the last of the kitchen surfaces clean, I nervously flitted a glance at the front door. It was almost eight. Usually at this point, Lena allowed me to change so I could look 'normal' when Claudia came home. I was so worried that she would walk in any second now, only to experience the nightmarish vision of her husband dressed in women's clothes.

Lena, however, didn't seem to care today.

Well, the worst-case scenarios aren't exactly tipped in my favor, I thought. The worst for Lena was that she could get fired. But for me? I didn't even want to think about Claudia finding out what I'd done. Knowing her, it was extremely likely that it would put an end to our marriage.

Of course, Lena didn't have proof. I tried to tell myself that at first— that I could always claim she was lying. I could just deny it till the end, and it wasn't like she could whip out video evidence of what I'd done that day. But I knew in my gut I didn't have the balls to lie my way through what would be a very thorny confrontation with my wife.

Lena, on the other hand, was an extremely good liar. The contrast between her once-bright and friendly personality and the bitchy attitude she had now was enough evidence of her acting skills. She could definitely play the victim part well if she needed to.

It was easier—and safer—for me to just submit.

After all, all she was asking me to do was crossdress and clean for her, right? She was just taking advantage of the situation and of course my stupidity. I wasn't sure why the maid's costume was necessary, but I probably guessed she wanted to humiliate me, just like how I'd humiliated her that day. The punishment fit the crime, didn't it? And yet, I had a sinking feeling that *something* was different about our arrangement, and there was something different about *her*. Lena was so smooth, so *seductive*, it was almost like she'd done it before—to another unsuspecting man who had a lot to lose.

"Your wife is going to be late," Lena announced, swiping a fingertip off the kitchen counter to check how I'd done. "She texted me an hour ago."

Relief flooded through me, but then I felt a pang of irritation. Since when did Claudia text Lena instead of me? Needless to say, she loved her.

I pushed down my maid's skirt, which had a habit of riding up my thighs. "What time is she coming home?"

"She won't be home for dinner. That's what she said."

"Okay."

Lena smiled.

God. She made me feel so different. So alive.

She knew exactly what she was doing.

"Let's go upstairs," she said.

My eyes widened. "Really?"

"Really. Come on."

I followed her to my bedroom, feeling flushed and full of adrenaline. But when we got there, she traipsed straight into the bathroom. It was sparkling. Squeaky clean. I'd only spent two hours scrubbing every surface the day before. She pulled up the toilet seat and made a face before going over to the bathtub. "I think you can do better than this, Mrs. Martin," she said, her voice full of mock encouragement. "Did you use the baking soda?"

I couldn't have felt more stupid. *Did I really think she'd come onto me?* "I did," I said meekly.

"Still dirty," she said, showing me the fingertip she'd just swiped on the inside of the tub. She grabbed me by my shoulder and pulled on my tight maid's top, hauling me over to the rim. Then she threw me a sponge. "I'm not going to have your wife thinking I don't know how to scrub a fucking tub."

I took a deep breath and started scrubbing at the invisible dirt.

The doorbell rang. My heart stopped completely for a second, and I thought I might black out. Claudia was here early and I had less than a minute to get out of the uniform and the wig or I would be in some very hot water. I looked at Lena, pleading with my eyes, but she just gave me another one of her sexy little smiles before her gaze traveled down my body. Did she like to see me like this—all helpless and scared? Her gaze fell on my legs and my heart skipped a beat. I hadn't even realized I was perched at the end of the tub with my legs crossed daintily like a woman…

"Anybody home?"

It took me a second to recognize who it was. Lena's boyfriend, Robbie. He was a blonde-haired dude who wore earrings on both ears and was about a year younger than her—and obviously unemployed. The last time he'd come over they'd ended up having sex on the couch underneath a blanket while I broke my back scrubbing the kitchen floor right next to them.

"We're up heeeere!" Lena sang.

Robbie walked into the bathroom a minute later. I was still sitting on the tub, but my hand was trembling as I held onto the sponge.

"Looking hot today, Mrs. Martin," Robbie said, licking his lips wickedly while he took me in. Then he laughed, and of course Lena laughed too.

This is my house, I thought bitterly, though I couldn't help blushing. *They're in my property doing whatever the hell they want to right under my nose and they still don't give a fuck.*

They started making out in front of me. Robbie yanked down the straps of Lena's overalls and the next thing I knew, her breasts were being coddled and massaged by Robbie's hungry fingers. I felt my insides quiver a little with excitement.

Good god, I thought. *what wouldn't I do to make that beautiful creature hold me…touch me…kiss me?*

I couldn't let Lena know how much I wanted her, though. I was still being punished for what I'd done earlier, and there was a part of me that wanted to prove to her I didn't just see her as a sex object. As ridiculous as it sounded, I still wanted to gain our maid's respect. Maybe—over time—she could see I was a good dude and we didn't need to resort to sketchy tactics.

"Are you having nasty thoughts about my boyfriend?" Lena said. "You are, aren't you!" She threw a disgusted look at me and turned to Robbie. "Let's get out of here."

Robbie laughed and hurried toward me. With one easy move he pushed me into the tub. I squeaked like an outraged cat and he just started laughing even harder.

So much for respect…

I could hear them making out again. The mattress springs groaned as they fell onto my bed and got ready for a round of passionate fucking.

Depressed, I hauled myself out of the tub and went back to cleaning.

CHAPTER 2

THAT NIGHT, MY WIFE TOLD ME the worst news possible.

She was going to leave for a one-day business trip.

"We have a new opportunity to pitch at a multinational," she said, tap-tapping on her phone to someone on her team. "If I pull this through it could mean a big bonus for us. We could go take a vacation in Thailand or something."

"But do you *have* to go?" I asked. All I could think of was Lena having me all to herself without the threat of Claudia coming home. I'd have to do a fuckton of housekeeping and…and what else? I almost shuddered to think what Lena would do to me.

"Babe," Claudia said, looking a little surprised. "Are you worried about something? You know you can tell me."

That was one of my wife's favorite phrases. *You know you can tell me anything!* It was also a big fat lie. It was almost funny how open-minded Claudia thought she was, when she had a hissy fit the one time she thought I was talking to an ex behind her back (I wasn't, and I'm still not sure to this day how she even got the idea).

"If it makes you feel better," Claudia continued. "I told Lena she can do a little deep cleaning while I'm away. It'll be a full day gig for her—wash the curtains, get the garage organized, that sort of thing. I love going away just to come back to a clean house." Her attention wavered for a split-second as her phone beeped. "Oh, and she said her boyfriend wouldn't mind coming over to help her out, and I agreed because they could get double the work done. If you want him to do a few errands like get you lunch or something I'm sure they wouldn't mind."

"I don't know," I said sulkily, feeling like a kid who'd had his lollipop taken away and stomped on. "I kind of wanted to have the house to myself."

"And do what?" Claudia asked, sharply this time. "You always have the house to yourself, Shane." She stood up and yawned. "I think I'm going to call it a night. Tomorrow's going to be a long day. You coming, babe?"

"Yeah," I muttered.

It was going to be a heck of a long day, alright.

***

Lena came over at ten the next morning, singing under her breath. She was wearing a pink tank top and gray sweatpants that looked like they were three sizes too big. She still looked amazing.

She whistled when she saw me. Wanting to get off on the right foot, I was already dressed in my maid's uniform and had fixed up my wig.

"Hello, Mrs. Martin," she said, her eyes still transfixed on my legs. "Did Claudia have a good flight?"

"Yes," I said. "She's in her hotel room now. Resting for an

hour or so before they travel for the pitch."

"Great. I hope you're ready for a good day of deep cleaning," Lena said, stepping past me into the living room.

"Where's Robbie? Isn't he coming to help?"

Lena turned around and slapped her hand down hard on my mouth. An instant surge of electricity shot through me, making every hair on my body stand on edge. She was touching me. Her soft palm smelled sweet, like one of Claudia's really nice hand creams.

I tried to speak, wondering what I'd done to cause an outburst so quickly but I was drowning in those big pretty eyes.

"Look," Lena said, her face coming so close to me her lips were almost touching my cheek. "First of all, I'm not Lena to you. Not today. I'm *Mistress,* and that's what you'll call me. Second of all, questions get directed from *me* to *you,* not the other way around. Do you understand what I'm saying? This isn't a game, Mrs. Martin. I mean business."

Cold shivers ran through me. What the hell was going on? Did Lena want to turn this into something sexual?

"Well?"

"I understand, Mistress," I mumbled into her mouth, feeling the top of my lip start to sweat.

"Good. Very good," Lena said. Then she looked at me sternly. "Why do you care so much about my boyfriend? Do you need a cock to look at?"

The way she'd said 'cock' had mine rustling inside my panties. "No, n-not at all, Mistress," I stuttered.

She gave me a hard look and then she was staring at my legs again. I felt them go all wobbly and for a second I thought I'd lose my balance.

"I want you to strip."

What?

"Lena, why are you…" I started, and this time she straight up slapped me on the mouth to get me to stop speaking.

"I hope you don't have memory loss, pea brain, because that's going to make things a lot harder for me here. What did I just say?"

By that time I was already imagining it. Stripping down and showing Lena my body. My cheeks got hot. I had no doubt she would make fun of it. I wasn't all that attractive, and didn't have any muscles to speak of. I was a lot more than a little out of shape.

And oh god—what if she wanted me to *strip* strip? As in…bare it all?

"We can start with the dress."

Jesus. She really did mean it all.

She had to be getting some kind of sexual satisfaction out of this, I thought. Why else would she be doing this? I couldn't deny that I was excited about that. Did she like dominating me? For a second I had the ludicrous thought of fapping to the fantasy of Lena tormenting and humiliating me. But why the fuck would I—when it was actually *happening* to me today?

Standing right under the AC vents, I shivered. "Right here…Mistress?"

Lena considered this. "We can go to your room."

In the bedroom, Lena just stood there again, arms crossed, leaning back with one knee up and one foot resting on the wall. I pulled all my hair to the front—the wig she had me put on was blonde and ridiculously shiny—and put my arms behind me to get to the zipper. I had the sudden, startling sense that we were *alone*. Completely alone, our bodies just inches away from each other. She had the whole day to do anything she wanted and nothing was really going to stop her.

I was completely at my hot maid's mercy.

CHAPTER 3

UNDER LENA'S GAZE, I FELT THE WARM BUZZ of desire spread down my body and pool downwards into my groin. I took a deep breath and tugged at the zipper. I got naked as if I was in a trance. First the braless dress slipped down my legs, and then, eventually, so did the matching black panties I was wearing underneath.

I covered up my crotch with both hands and looked at Lena expectantly. She'd caught a better glimpse of my cock this time—there was no doubt about that. Did she like what she saw?

Silently, she made me follow her to the bathroom again, where she started going through the drawers. She found a tube of Claudia's dark red lipstick, applied it, and then stepped back to admire herself. And I was still there naked, watching her go through my wife's things like they were her own.

A minute later she tossed something my way. It was a half-used tube of Veet.

"Do you know what that is?" Lena asked.

I was trying to hide my crotch again with one arm. "Uh, it's hair removal cream, Mistress."

"Do you know how to use it?"

I swallowed. "I could figure it out, I'm sure."

"Go for it, then," Lena said.

"How…" I started, not exactly sure what to do next. Did she want me to get rid of my hair everywhere? Why? What was she getting out of it? What would I tell Claudia once she was back?

Lena must've read my thoughts, because she said, "Use your wife's razor for the more sensitive parts. The Veet can go on your arms, legs, and underarms. I want everything clean, back and front. No questions." She slipped a shower cap over my wig and pointed to the walk-in shower. "I think it's best if you do less thinking and more doing."

Slowly, I went past her and into the shower. I had the weird feeling she was looking at my ass. I even got the feeling she might reach out and spank it. But she didn't. Was I disappointed? Of course I was. Other than those glorious few seconds she had her hand clamped onto my mouth, Lena had refused to touch me. This whole thing was fucking strange. I couldn't tell if she was disgusted by me or attracted to me.

I let the hot water soak over me and pinched my nose as the pungent smell of the hair remover took over the shower. I tried to get rid of my leg hair with a steady hand, but my fingers were shaking. I could hear Lena pissing behind me, but with the steam of the shower I couldn't see anything. *Less thinking, more doing.* I refused to look at the clumps of my hair trailing down the drain. Once I was done with my armpits, legs, and arms, I picked up Claudia's razor that was hanging off the shower caddy. With it I finished the hair removal job, making sure to groom my crack and balls as well as I could.

When I stepped out, Lena wasn't there. I toweled myself off and wrapped the towel around myself. I could hear Lena singing under her breath from my wife's walk-in closet.

She was holding one of Claudia's bras. It was a purple push-up one that had those humongous cushiony cups.

"Do you fuck her while she wears this?" Lena asked, not looking at me.

I was stunned by the question, though of course I shouldn't have been. Lena was definitely breaking the ice today.

I cleared my throat. "Not that particular one, no, Mistress. If I remember correctly."

"So you've fucked her while she wears a bra?"

"I have, Mistress."

"What's the kinkiest thing you've ever done with her?"

I had to pause and think. "Claudia's not really the kinky type, Mistress. We had sex with the balcony door open while on vacation in Greece. But we didn't realize it until after the fact..."

"Holy shit," Lena said, rolling her eyes. "No wonder Claudia looks like a bee stung her all the time. She needs someone to give her a good pounding."

"We...we don't have sex that often anymore," I admitted. "She's always wiped out when she comes home. It's like she's married to her work."

"She's a workaholic, huh?" Lena said, and for once I thought her face softened.

"Yeah."

She motioned to me to get rid of the towel, and I did, somehow now feeling more comfortable in front of her. She slipped the purple bra through my arms and fixed the hooks from the back. I was so fucking happy she was touching me again that I didn't care what she was doing. She filled out the cups with two pairs of Claudia's stockings. Then she stepped back to inspect her work.

"I mean," she said absent-mindedly. "If you're not happy anymore, why are you still married to her?"

I didn't have an answer. "It's not that easy. I still love her. And she loves me. She works hard for both of us."

Lena tossed me the matching pair of panties.

"I think you're a kinky person, Shane Martin," she said while I put them on. "Aren't you?"

I felt my face grow as hot as a furnace.

"I think you wanted to get caught that day," she accused me, dropping down her sweatpants and exposing her panties. She took one of Claudia's skirts—an old one I hadn't seen her wear in years—and shrugged them on. "I saw you looking at me. Trying so hard not to cross the line, but you just couldn't control yourself, could you? Some sick part of you wanted me to see your pathetic excited little cock as you jerked yourself off."

That wasn't the exact truth, but my throat had gone dry and I didn't really care to correct her. Looking for something to do while she hooked and zipped up my wife's skirt, I went to secure the rest of my maid's uniform, which was draped over one of the closet chairs.

Lena stopped me.

I looked down to see where she'd touched my arm, and I shivered all over again.

"No. This is all you'll be wearing today," she said.

My mouth gaped open. I couldn't believe what I was hearing.

Lena looked up and down my lingerie-clad body with a sly little grin. My *hairless* body. "You're much better to look at this way."

Something sprang to life inside me when she said that.

Fuck me. That was hot.

Lena let go of me and giggled. I felt myself melt to the floor. She was joking. Of course she was joking. With my hands shaking, I stepped into the maid's dress and zipped it up. The top was much tighter and just barely held me in with the humongous stuffed bra I was wearing. Lena dabbed some of Claudia's makeup on me—a little face powder, red lipstick, a dusting of blush, some bronzy eyeshadow—and made me wear a pair of black stilettos that were *really* tight. Then she spritzed some of Claudia's perfume on the side of my neck.

"You should watch porn with her," Lena said, while she brushed out my wig and handled a curler just on the ends.

Excuse me? I tried not to fidget. "Watch porn," I repeated dumbly. Why was she teasing me like this?

"Robbie and I watch porn together all the time," Lena said. "He picks out stuff he likes and I do the same, then we kind of do a marathon viewing together. It's like the easiest way to get turned on. I mean, who *doesn't* get turned on watching porn?"

"What, uh, kind of stuff do you like?" I blurted out, then quickly added, "Mistress?"

Lena didn't answer at first. Then she just muttered, "Nothing you would know," and left it at that. Like she thought I was too boring or stupid to get it.

My stomach was twisting itself into knots. She was acting like she hated my guts but then she was dishing me marriage advice. She was talking about porn and fucking Robbie and me fucking my wife and how much better I looked in a bra and panties. Lena's beauty was really my curse. It was like I was walking straight into a pit of quicksand but I couldn't do anything about it.

When she was done with my hair and I got to look at myself in the mirror I finally got it. What she'd done to me. She'd objectified me, just like I'd objectified her. I wasn't Shane anymore. I'd become the sexy maid with the big tits and long legs and the slutty high heels, only there to be used or toyed around with. *Her* maid.

Lena grabbed one of Claudia's fluffy robes and tied it around herself.

Stop, I thought. *Take that off. I want to see your body too.*

But our playtime was over.

"Time for your chores, Mrs. Martin," Lena said. She started the dreaded timer on her watch. "Washing curtains takes longer than you think, so you're going to get started on that first. Hurry the fuck up. You've got a lot to do."

As we walked downstairs—more like Lena walked and I scraped along the floor in my heels—I had the distinct feeling that Robbie was never going to come. Lena's plan was for me to do the work of two people and get rewarded. Nerves fluttered through me as I realized we were just getting started. I was excited, yes, but also anxious. *Very* anxious.

What else was the day going to hold?

What else was Lena going to do to me?

CHAPTER 4

FOR THE REST OF THE AFTERNOON, Lena made herself comfortable on the couch, calling some of her friends and watching Netflix while I got to work. She was back to being bitchy, ignoring me completely other than to yell at me about spots I'd missed or spending too long on a job.

To make matters worse, I was sweating like hell not even an hour into Lena's job. My maid's uniform was hot, my chest felt hot inside the bra, and my wig was overheating. I felt like a freak wearing makeup and heels and just having to act like a woman for Lena, but even more than that, I desperately wanted things to go back to how they were, when she'd teased me and joked around with me and done my hair.

I needed her to touch me again.

In the evening, Claudia called and asked me how everything was going. I snuck into the downstairs bathroom and said that everything was perfect.

"Did Lena and Robbie do the garage yet?"

"Yes they did," I said. "And um, they washed the curtains and the windows."

Claudia sounded happy. "You know what, I just remembered something! The kitchen walls are getting a bit musty and they could do with, like, a good wash. Tell Lena to add it to the list. Robbie could do that."

I almost groaned out loud. "Okay."

"Just make sure they do a good job," Claudia said. "And keep an eye on 'em. They look like they could get a little rowdy, you know?" Then she giggled, and I heard someone else giggle in the background. Claudia giggled even harder.

"You sound drunk," I said flatly.

"I'm not drunk," Claudia said. "I'm having *fun*. The pitch went so well we're celebrating."

"Maybe when you come home we can do a celebration of our own," I said.

She giggled again. "I just don't want them having sex, like, on my bed. Or anywhere else in my house, for that matter. I like the girl but I don't know much about her boyfriend and he sounds like he could be a little quirky, don't you think? Shane…you *are* keeping an eye on them, aren't you?"

It was like she hadn't even heard me.

"Yeah, I am," I mumbled, flicking off a strand of yellow hair that had fallen over my eyes. "Whatever."

When the call was done I went back to the kitchen and continued mopping up the floor. But I just couldn't keep my mind on the job. I tried to speed up, worried that Lena would be pissed off at me again and that I'd never be able to repair our relationship. While I was breaking my back, Lena woke up from her nap, switched off the TV, and came to the kitchen. She had the funniest expression on her face, and I could feel her looking at me while I worked. More than looking, actually. *Staring.* At my thighs and my ass. At my enormous bust. I tried not to be so self-conscious, tried not to feel stupid and ridiculous as I moved around the floor, every one of my movements making me cringe inside.

"You can take a break from cleaning, sissy," Lena said.

I stared up at her.

"Thank you, Mistress," I finally said.

"Make me lunch."

I set the mop aside, washed my hands and opened the fridge, wondering what the heck I could make for Lena. She wasn't giving me any specific instructions. We had leftover lentil soup from two nights ago, but I wasn't sure whether she'd like it. I decided on making a ham sandwich with a fruit salad to accompany it.

Lena watched me quietly, leaning against the kitchen counter with her arms crossed as I prepared her meal. Her robe had fallen back and my wife's short skirt rode up, exposing the pink underwear that matched her tank top.

"Feed me a grape," she said suddenly.

I stopped short. I felt my face redden.

I clumsily reached for a grape but it fell, rolling onto the floor. I laughed awkwardly and reached for another one. Lena opened her mouth. Her lips swallowed my outstretched fingers and then she sucked, slowly, until the grape popped backward into her mouth.

"Another one," she said.

I fed her a second grape. And then another one. And another

one. Each time she just sucked it off my fingers. I was trying hard not to meet Lena's eyes but it was impossible not to do that when her fierce eyes were challenging me. The feel of her soft wet lips on my hand was turning me into a raging puddle of lust. I wanted her to kiss me all over with her wet pink mouth. I wanted her to be rough with me. I wanted her to rip my dress open. I wanted her to tease me and make me her woman forever. I wanted *her*.

When the last grape in the bowl disappeared in her mouth, Lena grabbed me by the shoulders and pushed me down to my knees. She hiked up her skirt and pulled down her panties and the next thing I knew, she was rubbing her swollen red clit.

Someone save me. Please...

Lena stared down at me as she widened her pussy lips with her fingers, showing me her dripping wet vagina. My cock jumped up, aching inside my wife's tight purple underwear. *Holy shit. I need to worship her.*

She pushed my head in between her legs.

I kissed her, letting my nose savor the soft scratch of her landing strip. Lena sighed. I straightened my neck and kissed the silver piercing on her belly button, then kissed all the way down to her clit again. I started sucking, trying to meet the same intense sexual energy she had as she fed herself off my fingers. My heart was practically beating out of my chest and I trembled underneath the power of her strong legs.

Lena pulled her skirt up even further and began wiping her juices on my face. She was breathing hard, her hips pushing into me, and then she was moaning. I rubbed my fingers up and down her gaping hole as I pleasured her clit. Smelling her. Drugging myself with her hot scent. When I couldn't wait any longer, I started finger-fucking her, slurping up the juices that were dribbling out.

"I've been watching you all day," she hissed at me. "I know what you're doing. Trying to get me to come after you when you're bending over with that ass on show for me. Following my orders with that slutty skirt on like you're the world's most obedient sissy. I've seen you in a fucking bra, bitch. Look at your fucking tits. Look at them. Honestly, what did you think would happen to me?"

My ears turned pink. It was almost shocking how well Lena knew how to push my buttons.

"Fucking answer me."

"I didn't know I was doing that, Mistress. I'm so sorry. I didn't mean to…"

"Answer me like a fucking girl!"

My breath hitched. "Please forgive me, Mistress," I said, in a quiet, high-pitched voice that made me cringe. "I'm trying. I really want to make you feel good. I want…"

"I don't care about what you want," Lena said. I dared to look at her, and her eyes were like black ice. She rammed my head into her pussy again. When she spoke again it was like she was spitting every word out. "Taste me. Taste me like I'm the hottest chick in the fucking world. And don't even breathe until I'm done."

You are, I wanted to say. *You're the most beautiful girl I've ever seen.* But I couldn't speak. I could only lick.

Lena's phone rang. The trills echoed in the kitchen, causing me to roll backward. The name flashed across the screen as she took it out of her robe.

Claudia Martin.

"Hurry up, sissy," Lena hissed.

I snuck my head in between her legs again. But the ringing was making me lose my concentration. I was annoyed at Claudia for ruining a good moment. Why did she have to call Lena now? Of course she wanted to check whether I'd passed her stupid message along.

The ringing stopped. Then it started again. *Damn you, Claudia.* I furiously licked Lena and then stuck my tongue inside her pussy, praying that I could make her cum soon.

Lena reached down and pinched the flesh of my shoulder. I cried out in pain.

"Don't drool all over me, idiot!" The sudden anger in her voice was making my blood curdle. "Don't you know how to eat a girl out? God I wish I could fuck you right now so you'd learn a good lesson. "

CHAPTER 5

MY HEART SANK TO MY FEET. I licked my lips, trying to think up an apology that could actually work. Lena's phone was *still* ringing. I tried to say something but she pushed me off.

"Fuck off!" she yelled.

The moment she swiped the phone open to answer Claudia, her personality changed.

"Everything good?" Claudia's muffled voice buzzed in our ears.

"Yes, of course," Lena said sweetly. "I was just sweeping the front porch. We're making great progress, Mrs. Martin."

"Great. How about Robbie? What has he done so far?"

"He's been *so* helpful." I tried to get up but her foot slammed onto my stomach, holding me still. "He's, uh, dusting right now. I can't wait for you to see the home when you come back, Mrs. Martin."

"Did Shane tell you about the walls?"

"Walls?" Lena asked, narrowing her eyes at me.

As the conversation continued I could see her becoming more

and more agitated. When Claudia finally hung up a horrible silence filled the air. I didn't dare move.

Lena threw her phone on the counter and went through the kitchen cabinets. She took out a big roll of brown packing tape and turned to me.

"No wonder your wife doesn't want to fuck you," Lena said softly. She knelt down and tore the roll open, cutting off a piece with her teeth.

Time slowed down to nothing as she taped my feet down onto the floor by my ankles. She did the same thing to my wrists, stretching my arms out behind my head. Each solid *rrrrrip* of that tape with her canines made my insides squirm. The smell of lavender Pine-Sol from the freshly mopped floor was making me feel light-headed.

The fluffy robe fell to the floor beside me, followed by Lena's pink underwear. Then she squatted down and straddled my face with her asshole practically brushing against my nose and her hands gripping onto my stomach.

"Fuck you, loser," she whispered. "I bet you fuck your wife like a sissy faggot. If you can even call it fucking." Her nails were drumming across my cleavage. I squirmed some more, feeling powerless with my useless limbs as she probed my body like she owned it. She squeezed my breasts in a rush, almost impatiently, like she'd been waiting to do it all day but had painfully held back. Incredibly, it was like she was as enamored with my fake breasts as I was with hers…and it was tripping me up.

"See, the thing is…" she continued, her horny, sultry voice sending my heartrate through the roof. "You don't even look like a man to me. You're just a kinky sissy who wants to wear slutty bras and short skirts. I know that. You don't have to tell me. The only way you can tempt a girl is if you look all cute in panties and show off that sissy ass of yours."

I moaned. I felt so helpless.

"You know, you suck at licking a girl out but I bet you can give good sloppy blowjobs to a guy with big balls and a big dick," Lena said. "It's a good thing I'm going to be teaching you how to please a woman. Consider it a favor from me."

Her fingers kept clawing at my cleavage, as if she was driven by this insane primal need to use me for some depraved shit that had been hiding inside her head for years. Like my feminized body was so sexy she couldn't control those urges. Still, I couldn't help feeling like Franken-freak. After all, *she* was the one who had created…this…this woman? No. I wasn't a woman. I was a bitch. Her bitch. A *sissy*. And I…I liked it. I wanted *more* of whatever she'd done to me.

Jesus. What had I become?

"Take a deep breath, sissy. You'll need it."

Lena made this scary guttural coughing sound and spat on her hand. With the spit she reached underneath my bra and began rubbing my nipples. *Holy shit.* No one had ever played with my nipples before. Another moan escaped my throat. I sounded needy. Desperate.

"How does this feel?" she asked.

"Amazing, Mistress." I murmured. "Fuck, what are you doing to me…"

"Make me feel the same way."

She started bouncing her ass on top of my face. From my vantage point, her thighs looked strong enough to crush me.

Each time she whacked onto my face, I tried to take a deep breath. I was high on her natural scent.

When she sat back on my face again and stayed put, I started licking her furiously.

"You need to *think* with your mouth, bitch," Lena rasped. "Suck my clit like it's a cock."

I slowed down and started suckling her hot nub, which was getting wetter by the second. I was sure I was in some kind of fever dream—I really *couldn't* be restrained to the kitchen floor and licking my hot maid's pussy. This was beyond anything I could've ever dreamt or fantasized about.

Lena was pinching my nipples now. Each pinch was like an orgasmic electric shock straight to my brain. With my arms outstretched I had the weird feeling my chest was propped unnaturally upward and that was why I was so sensitive. I trembled hopelessly underneath her, drenched in her juices and kept my rhythm. I could feel my cock tenting under my skirt but Lena wasn't giving it any attention.

It was like I didn't even have a cock.

She suddenly let go of my breasts and turned around, flashing her glorious pussy shot in my face. She spread her thighs wide open and leaned back, resting her head on my groin.

"Eat my cunt, bitch," she ordered.

Then she was riding my face hard, and I almost couldn't breathe, and I felt like I was drowning in the deep sea but I kept going, wanting to not just be good but *amazing* so she'd never forget me.

"Oh fuck!" Lena cried out. "Keep doing that! Keep doing that! Don't fucking stop!"

She climaxed less than ten seconds after that. I didn't let go of her while she orgasmed, ignoring my numbed jaw and exhausted tongue to keep Mistress happy. Her slippery thighs twitched powerfully while I kept flapping my tongue and sucking her juices off of her. Slowly, eventually…she calmed down and fell silent. The only sounds I could hear then was her soft, sweet breathing and my beating heart.

Lena stood up and fixed up my dress top before getting rid of the tape binding me to the floor.

"I'll have my lunch now," she said, her face painfully emotionless as she wiped herself with a wad of paper towels and threw the used ones at me. "And then you can go back to cleaning."

CHAPTER 6

I HAD TO FIX MORE THAN MY DRESS top after that. After serving
Lena's lunch, I quickly escaped to the bathroom and washed my
face and straightened out my wig. I could see how exhausted I
looked in the mirror. My body felt like a log…yet I'd never felt
so alive. I opened up one of the drawers and found the little travel
pouch that Claudia kept stocked whenever we went on mini-
vacations. It just had some of her essentials—a small face powder
with a separate applicator, a blush kit, a lipstick, and some gloss.

I studied my pale, makeup-less face. It looked so wrong.

I applied a little of Claudia's pink lipstick and rubbed my lips
together, then went ahead and patted my T-zone with the powder
and brushed some rouge on my cheeks. I finished off with two
coatings of the light, clear gloss. I did all this sort of in a daze—
not really sure why I was doing it. At least not consciously. But
the truth was there and I probably felt it only deep in my bones,
and the truth was that I needed to be feminine to make Lena
horny.

I made my way back to the kitchen. Lena was enjoying her

lunch. She didn't talk to me. When she was done and we got back to my chores, she still kept ignoring me. The only time she spoke was to give me orders or to yell at me for something I hadn't done. Even after everything we'd been through I couldn't help feeling like a failure.

What was it going to take? I thought. We still had a whole half-day left. Claudia was going to be back early the next morning, and I hated thinking about that. I just didn't want our day to end on this weird, cold, passionless note.

Unfortunately, as the hours slowly but surely ticked by, Lena's mood spiraled down. By evening she'd uncovered a problem. And it was a big problem. There was just no way I could do everything on Claudia's list in the time we had left, especially with her adding more stuff in since she'd left. Lena would have to pitch in.

By eight, she was growing increasingly restless. I tried to do my best, washing, scrubbing, wiping everything she'd told me but we'd barely done half the tasks on her to-do list. I hoped she'd have no choice but to join me. To finish this as a team.

"I'm meeting friends at a bar in an hour," she finally admitted when we were in one of the upstairs bathrooms. "And we still have so much to do."

"Sorry to hear that, Mistress," I said, trying to sound sympathetic. "We could...make something up for Claudia. An excuse."

"No."

I'd known that wasn't an option deep down too. To do that would be too risky. Claudia would catch on to the fraud that she was, and this time it wouldn't just be me getting into trouble.

I got down on my knees and started scrubbing the bottom of the shower glass with my sponge. Lena was by the sink, inspecting what I'd just cleaned. I saw her swipe a fingertip across the bottom of the sink. My heart sank, because her finger was full of dust. "Where did this come from?" she asked, her voice shrill. "I don't think you've done anything right, sissy."

I was sure that Lena was on the verge of a panic attack. Did she really think that she could pull it off, with us playing around and having just me do all the work? It reminded me that she was still young. Still naive. I hated seeing her like this. I wanted to do the right thing, make her feel better...but the problem was I didn't know what the right thing was. Hug her? Kiss her? Console her? Tell her I could somehow find a way to pacify my wife— even if that definitely wasn't true?

"Could you see if Robbie can come over for a couple of hours?" I asked gingerly. *Or you could, like, you know...help me out here?*

"I can't," she said, but she didn't elaborate any further.

"Maybe you should've been honest with Claudia in the first place," I said.

Maybe it was a stupid thing to say. What I'd meant was that *we* should've just told Claudia that there was no way Lena and Robbie could get everything she wanted done in the hours they had.

It was absolutely the wrong thing to say.

Lena's head whipped around and I knew I'd done it.

What was it going to take for her to want me again?

"I can't fucking deal with you right now," she said and stomped out of the bathroom.

I tried getting up and racing after her but every muscle in my legs had turned to stone. So I just balled myself up in the corner of the shower and waited.

I'd pissed Lena off. I was sweating, and my wig was overheating yet again. And yet I was shivering. I dipped my hand into my bra and pinched my right nipple, hard. My mouth was dry but I could still taste Lena. Something about this situation was turning me on. I could feel Lena's rage, wherever she was in my house at that moment. I had no idea what she was thinking or planning to do, but I somehow knew she'd be after me again. Despite the fact I felt terrible for her, I was rejoicing in the fact that she was lusting after me.

I snuck my fingers inside my panties and began rubbing myself. I marveled at how small my dick really was. Maybe it didn't deserve to be called a dick.

I bit my tongue so I wouldn't moan out loud.

The feeling of slipping into that deep pit of quicksand was back again, but it was way more intense now. I knew I needed to submit. Fully. Completely.

I wanted to lose myself in Lena.

Feel her rage on my body.

So I prayed that it would happen.

CHAPTER 7

I WAS PLAYING WITH MY SMALL dicklette when Lena returned. She stopped short and stared at me. I found it amusing that this was actually the second time she'd caught me this way, and I made no attempt to cover myself up this time or flee like a coward. Lena began chewing her lip and I could feel her pure, overwhelming lust. I'd just confirmed to her what she'd suspected all along—that I was a kinky girl and I secretly loved her cruelty.

"Get up, slut," she hissed.

When I did she whacked me against the shower wall and forcefully stretched my hands out. She'd brought along the roll of packing tape. She began winding it around my wrists, binding them tightly together, and then positioned me with my face turned toward the wall. She slapped more tape to restrain my wrists to the tiles above my head.

"This should shut you up." The tape screeched as she rolled out some more and smacked a strip right over my mouth. After that came another layer of tape and then another. Sealing me tight

179

so I couldn't speak.

I tried to moan.

My wrists were already hurting as I held on tight just by those heavy strips of tape. I could almost taste the dew on the shower tiles and the faint whiff of bathroom cleaner saturated the space. We were in the smallest bathroom in the house—the one that connected our office and one of the guest bedrooms, and that forced Lena to basically squash me into the wall.

I felt light and breathless but I was losing my inhibitions.

I had no idea what she was going to do to me.

Lena pulled my skirt up and whacked my body against the tiles so I'd stop squirming. God, she was strong. I felt her hand on my right ass cheek. My *bare* ass cheek. And then she was senselessly squeezing it, over and over again. It definitely hurt but I was instantly craving for more. Her hand shifted to my left cheek, her nails digging deep into my butt fat. Playing with it. Squeezing it. I was suddenly feeling giddy with euphoria.

"Look," she said, and her voice sounded so loud in my ears. "I don't care how you do it. It's not my problem. It's yours." She was spanking me then and my ass burned with each impact. "And by that I mean the house needs to be clean by the time your prissy wife comes home." She spanked me hard then squeezed my butt again, slinking so close from behind that I could feel her pussy lining up perfectly against my ass. "I'm not joking around, sissy. That's an order. I'm going to show you I'm not fucking around."

She whipped my head around and stared at me. I met her eyes with both fear and pure exhilaration on my face.

I nodded furiously.

Her hand was exploring my ass again and then I heard her spit.

Something warm and wet invaded my crack. Lena wrapped her arm around my waist and held me tight as she penetrated me with a finger.

I was sure I was going to pass out.

Lena dug into me as much as she could. But my hole was tight. Innocent and inexperienced. More spit followed, so much so that I felt like I was leaking from behind. She slowly started finger-fucking me, trying to get me dilated, burying her finger in the furthest it could go. I couldn't help but close my eyes and surrender to the feelings that were taking control of my body.

I heard her spit yet again, and the wetness landed directly on my butt this time. And then I felt something warm…damp…deliciously soft stick itself inside me.

Lena's *tongue*.

Instinctively, my arms jolted. I'd wanted to reach down and push my cheeks apart so I could show Lena what a slut I really was. But of course I couldn't. I couldn't move much at all in that cramped shower, couldn't even speak or moan, and that was when I felt really helpless. Everything was in Lena's control. I was just on the receiving end of her fantasy…

I held my breath and shivered as Lena licked and stimulated my asshole in an enraged state. All I could do was widen my legs to help open myself up for her. Less than a minute later, I could tell I was ready.

Lena abruptly let go of me.

"I'll be back," she said. "Don't move."

No! I wanted to scream. *Touch me! Touch me now!* I thought I'd go crazy if I didn't feel her mouth on me again, her soft yet strong arm holding me tight. But I was powerless here, so I waited until

Lena returned, keeping my legs stretched to hold my asshole open for her.

When I heard her come back in again I held my breath. Soon I felt her presence with me in the shower. My heart was racing but I couldn't bring myself to look at her.

"I'll let you in on a little secret," Lena whispered, leaning her weight against me, gyrating against my ass, until we were slowly swaying together with our legs intertwined like we were Bachata dancing or something. I waited for her to speak again. Her breath was hot and sweeping. Oddly comforting. Then something soft and slimy—like a snake—rubbed up and down my back.

"Feel that?" Lena murmured. "I found this in Claudia's closet."

When I looked down and saw what it was I almost recoiled in horror. It was a brown rubber dildo...it was dark...thick...veiny...and it was tied to Lena's hips expertly in a criss-cross pattern with a scarf. The way she'd strapped it onto herself gave away that she'd definitely done this before. Put a cock on herself.

This was *Claudia's?*

"Just what I thought," Lena said, and she laughed. "You didn't know your wife had this, did you? Just imagine...she fucked herself with this huge rubber dick while she deprived you of sex...how does that make you feel?"

The sting of hurt burned my eyelids. I felt a tear roll down my cheek.

Lena hugged me. "I'm sorry, sissy baby. I didn't mean to make you cry. We all have secrets..."

Then she was forcing me to arch my spine back and bump my

ass up for her. She began flapping my wife's dildo against my back entrance. The tip entered me with a short sting and as it further invaded my passage it stretched me. My dicklette bobbed wildly when she started fucking me and I felt my whole groin flex, a hot stream of precum oozing out of me.

I was sweating in the shower and so was Lena. We were both engulfed in this feverishly hot cloud of sexual yearning. As she pounded into me I realized I'd *definitely* underestimated Lena's strength. I wished I could see myself getting fucked in the ass wearing a maid's uniform. Damn, I even wished Claudia could see me now and realize what a kinky sissy slut her husband really was.

Each time the dildo hit me, my chest whacked against the wall and my ass jiggled. Lena pulled out and rubbed the dildo head roughly against my taint, teasing me cruelly. More precum dribbled out of me. *So* much precum. That was the point I knew I didn't have control over my body any longer. It was going to do what it had to do and all I could do was buckle myself up along for the ride.

When Lena thrust her cock into me again all I could feel was this blur of ecstasy. My asshole was stretching beyond what I ever thought was possible and my whole body felt weak. She upped the pace until she was fucking me with two pumps every second and my teeth were chattering. But never in a million years could I have guessed what she would do right after that...

Because the next thing I knew, I was floating. Lena had backed her knees against the wall and had lifted my thighs up into the air. I screamed into my gag as my entire weight glided onto her cock, burying it to the hilt.

"Feel that? Feel that deep inside your pussy?" Lena hissed. "Now you know I'm not fucking around. You'll put your pea brain to use and get me out of this mess because I need your wife's money. And I know you'll do it." She slammed into me, fucking me slowly and sensually. "You know how I know you'll do it? Because I know you want to see me again. I know that because you're so fucking boring and I'm the only exciting thing in your pathetic life."

And with that she reached around me and squeezed my cocklette. "Shoot it out, sissy. Shoot it all out now!"

I felt a wave building from deep within me. My balls groaned and shuddered as I burst into her hand, my asshole still thumping, still violated by Lena. Seeing my shameful milk collect in her palm and my scent fill pungently in the air was incredibly gratifying. Lena pumped my shaft, forcing every last drop out. It was a huge fucking load, white and milky and insanely thick.

Lena reached up with one hand and ripped the tape off my mouth. I gasped and heaved, allowing a lungful of air to enter my throat which was now as dry as sand. Then, with a smile playing on her lips, she dipped a finger into my puddle of cum and slithered it over my lips. I shivered, feeling it coat over my mouth like a thick gloss.

"You know you want to," she whispered.

Heart fluttering, I licked my lips and stared into her eyes. She stared into mine. She fed me the remaining cum, little by little, first smearing it over my lips then encouraging me to suck it in. I couldn't believe what I was doing but I wanted this moment to freeze so it could last forever. I was sad that Lena would be leaving me so soon. I didn't know how I was going to do it but I knew that somehow I'd get the house in shape. I would cover up her mess because she was right. She was the only exciting thing in my life.

"Don't swallow yet," she said, and pulled out for the final time.

She leaned closer and we kissed. We were sharing the sweet fruits of her labor. Her tongue felt magical on mine and I was ecstatic that she was tasting my sissy cum along with me. That meant something, didn't it? Lena pulled me closer and we both moaned at the same time. I was really on cloud nine and I didn't think I'd ever be ready to come back down to reality.

THE END

SISSIES IN HEAT
BROKEN BY MY BULLY

BROKEN BY MY BULLY

CHAPTER 1

TWELVE LONG YEARS. THAT WAS how long it had been since I'd packed my bags and got out of that place, never looking back. I'd made a promise to myself that I'd break my back to make sure I'd never have to return again, even if that meant cutting off what little family I had.

I'd kept that promise for more than a decade.

But now I was back.

I wouldn't have gone back if not for my aunt's wedding. My aunt Beth raised me after my mom died when I was eight. My dad's always been out of the picture—I like not to think about him much. Aunt Beth, Mom's sister, was a widow herself, so she basically took care of me like a single mom. When I left her at eighteen she started dating again and met Ricky, a gentle divorcé in his fifties who owned a nice woodworking shop and could take care of her for a change. I was elated for her when she told me they were finally going to get married, but when she sent through the wedding invitation I think she half-expected me to decline it. I'd never accepted any of her invitations over the years, always saying I was broke and couldn't afford a plane ticket until she just stopped asking altogether.

"Don't be a shitty person," my girlfriend Jadyn said when I told her about the wedding. "This woman single-handedly raised you and you're going to shun her off on the happiest day of her life? Seriously, Todd? I can't believe you've never met Ricky either."

"That's not true," I argued. "I've called them plenty of times. It's not like I've never kept in touch."

"It's not the same," she said coldly.

"Fine," I said, wincing. The memories of my hometown were already trying to claw their way back to the surface, but I refused to pay them any attention. Thinking about the past wasn't going to do me any good. I looked up at Jadyn's huge expectant eyes and forced a smile. "We're going."

Jadyn hugged me. "You need to call Beth right now," she said. "I'll look at ticket deals. We need to think about gifts too. Oh my god, what am I going to wear?" She drifted straight to her closet and began rummaging through her dresses.

She was clearly excited. Jadyn and I were at the point in our relationship where even the mere mention of a wedding could get her all worked up. It was kind of cute. Four years of steady courtship and there was nothing I wanted more than to call Jadyn *mine*, my wife. I was already looking at rings and planning a romantic surprise getaway for next year.

I couldn't wait to see those eyes light up once I put a ring on that finger.

But for now, I had another wedding to go to. Another wedding to be happy for. A part of me still couldn't believe I was actually going back, returning to the place that buried me under what were probably the darkest years of my life, where I was an outcast in every sense of the word. Younger Todd was skinny and had long hair that wasn't cut as often as it needed to be because he thought it'd distract from a face full of acne. Of course, the only thing the long hair did was exacerbate my skin condition and attract the bullies who wanted to pick on a girly-looking guy. The worst part was I had no real friends—the school I went to was small and everyone knew each other because their families hung out with one another. The only person who talked to me with any dignity was probably my English teacher, who was sweet and kind and exactly like Miss Honey from Matilda.

If I had had friends, I know it would've softened the blow of those years just a little bit. Maybe it wouldn't have impacted me so much, especially more than a decade later. Some of my bullies I actually didn't mind too much, in the sense I could shrug them off and still go about my day, knowing they tormented pretty much anyone who seemed even a little different. There was Max, who mostly tried to scare me and intimidate me after school, calling me his favorite names: girlie, shorty, or pussy. There was John, who once snatched my notebook full of the drawings I'd painstakingly done and half-flushed the pages down the toilet. And then there was Jared, who was maybe the worst out of that lot and had fun throwing whatever he was drinking that day at me, often soaking me from the waist down so I'd have to hurry home during breaks and change so I wouldn't miss yet another class.

The bully who outdid all of them, however—and the one I hated the most—was Shannon Kelley. I can still remember the sickening blood-like smell of the metal lockers as she pushed me up against them and spit in my face or stuck her chewing gum into my hair so I was forced to cut the strands off. She was hot, obviously, but she was also a great student and the fact that her dad knew the school principal allowed her to get away with almost anything. While my other bullies targeted many people, Shannon seemed hellbent on making just *my* life miserable. She'd call me every name in the book and get her girl gang to throw things at me in the lunchroom. She spread rumors that I gave my butt to any guy who could give me five bucks because I was that broke and desperate. And started a bunch of other rumors that made sure I kept being a complete loner.

Shannon made me feel worthless.

There was one memory, though, that outlasted all the others. That memory still remained so crisp I could convince myself that it just happened yesterday. There was a fire drill at school, and I was late to get out because I was in the bathroom. Once I'd done my business and stepped out, everyone else had assembled outside like planned. Everyone, that is, except for Shannon, who pushed me by my shirt to the room next to it...the girls' bathroom. It smelled badly of cigarette smoke, and I knew she'd probably been in there smoking all morning.

That was when I got really scared. It was just me and my worst bully together—alone—in our entire high school building.

Shannon was tall. Like 5'9" tall—she even did modeling as a part-time gig. And then there was me. Just a stump of a guy. She just stood over me like a tree for a while. She was wearing this pink top that showed off her midriff and a tight pink skirt. I remember thinking how perfect her body was in that moment of total fear. The wall was gross and sticky but I leaned back, causing her to move forward and bend down a bit. Even though it made zero sense, I thought she was bending down to kiss me. But of course that wasn't what she did. She stripped down, letting her top and skirt pile up on the floor before peeling off her panties. Then she stripped me down and made me wear them, watching intently as those tight pink bikini briefs cupped my cock as they slid past my hips. She took off her bra and made me wear that too. She fished out her phone and started snapping pictures of me.

I was so ashamed of what she'd done to me. She'd turned me into a girl. Just like that. I tried really hard to fight my erection as her gorgeous nude body swayed from side to side, capturing my humiliating moment from all angles.

After that day, I was worried sick, wondering when she'd unleash those pictures to everyone at school. I knew it was only a matter of time. At first I thought she'd release them that same week, concocting some kind of rumor like I'd snuck in and stole her underwear because I was that desperate for male attention. But even when nothing cropped up that week, I was far from relieved. When several weeks went by, I figured Shannon was just waiting for the perfect moment to out me and destroy me. But then a year came and went.

She never did release those pictures.

When she bullied me again, it was like nothing ever happened. Like she never dressed me up in her own bra and underwear. Like she never took pictures of it for proof, so she always, *always* had the power over me.

She never mentioned it again.

Even though the horrifying day I kept imagining would happen never did, the day she made me submit and wear her clothes was in many ways a turning point. I quickly lost count of the number of times I masturbated thinking about her towering over me, her body bared just for me. Her sharp eyes raking through my own naked body as I stood there waiting for her to tell me what to do. How amazing my cock actually felt inside the tightness of her panties. I would jerk myself off, feeling furious and miserable and ashamed and a million other things at once, letting myself feel what I'd tried so hard to constrain that day in the girls' bathroom.

I'd never kissed anyone, let alone had sex. That was probably the closest I'd ever been to a girl.

It just so happened she was my bully.

I knew—deep in my heart—that I had excited her. Even if she never showed any outward signs. She liked me being a girl *just for her*, even if it was just for a fleeting moment.

CHAPTER 2

FOUR MONTHS AFTER MY DECISIVE conversation with Jadyn, Ricky had come to pick us up from the station. He was exactly like I'd seen him in the pictures. He wrapped his arms around both of us and squeezed us into a big hairy bear hug.

"Good to see you boy!" he said, and thumped me on my back.

As we sped through the quiet streets in his Ford F-150, I couldn't help but notice that everything looked the same. The same tacky looking convenience stores, the teenage hotshots sat smoking on the curbs, kids playing in the muddy parks, scruffy old people lining up in front of the post office. The sky was always a gray even when it was sunny. The past was still in the air. I could smell it. It was like my hometown had frozen time, waiting for me to come back.

Jadyn squeezed my hand the entire way, keeping her eyes peeled even though a long flight plus a three-hour bus ride had wiped her out.

I sucked in a breath when we turned into the driveway of Aunt Beth's house. My childhood home, just a decade older. It seemed exactly the same, other than a little fading and graying. The moment Ricky cut off the engine the front door opened and there was Aunt Beth, beaming.

She waved her arms at me in an excited frenzy. I rushed toward her and hugged her. She hugged me back for the longest time. It felt amazing, but I couldn't ignore the guilt that was creeping up on me. Aunt Beth was once the most important person in my life, and I'd waited too long to see her in person.

"And this must be your fiancée," Aunt Beth said, her eyes twinkling.

"Uh, my girlfriend," I corrected her awkwardly, then mumbled under my breath, "But yeah, soon enough…"

"Todd's told me so much about you!" Jadyn said, hugging her too. "You shouldn't have let us stay in your home. You must be so busy!"

"Nonsense. I will not have you staying into a hotel room like a pair of strangers," Aunt Beth said. "You're a very pretty one. Todd's lucky to have you."

Jadyn blushed.

Ricky and I took our suitcases inside and we quickly made ourselves home in the cozy kitchen. Aunt Beth had already laid the table for lunch since she figured we must have been hungry after traveling. She'd made her chicken pot pie with an olive salad and her delicious layered jelly to go along with it.

"So tell me more about your fabulous fiancée," Aunt Beth said brightly as we all dug in. "How did you two meet?"

"Oh, at work," I said.

"Todd got drunk on a work trip and he asked me out," Jadyn said.

Ricky raised an eyebrow. "I'd like to hear that story."

I reddened. "It didn't happen *quite* like that," I said. "I'd been meaning to ask her out and it just so happened the trip was perfect timing. Okay, maybe I was a little drunk. But Jadyn told me she'd had a crush on me for ages so it all worked out."

Jadyn pinched my cheeks and put on her private baby voice. She was obviously comfortable enough to put on that voice knowing full well it would make me horny. "Of course I had a crush on him. How could I have not with these cute little cheeks?"

Aunt Beth laughed. "Todd was even cuter when he was younger. As cute as a button. Now he's become a *man*." She grabbed my bicep with an amused expression like she was checking how big my muscles were. "So do you still work at...what was that place? The community arts center? You used to be a coordinator there if I remember correctly."

"No, it's been a couple of years since I left that job," I said. I cleared my throat. "I'm now a financial advisor. At a wealth management firm."

Ricky grinned. "A pity I couldn't get hold of some of that advice for the wedding."

Aunt Beth rolled her eyes. "If it was up to Ricky he'd be standing up there in just shorts and a see-through tank top," she said. Her eyes met mine again. "It's a shame that your old friends all seem to have moved out. You could've had a reunion."

I dug into my layered jello and took a big bite, feeling my heart clench tight. "Yeah. Shame."

"Oh, except for Shannon," Aunt Beth said, clapping a hand over her forehead like she'd just remembered her. "Shannon

Kelley! Do you remember her, Todd? She was your friend! Now she's all grown up. Married a musician. Has a sweet baby boy and everything. Such a beautiful family."

I bit down hard on my tongue to stop myself from saying something I would regret. I couldn't believe my aunt had forgotten that Shannon used to be my bully. I'd always told her what I could, but I had to leave out the grisly details for her own sanity. But she knew Shannon was one of the worst. She knew I *hated* her.

Maybe she thought I'd moved on.

After lunch, Aunt Beth showed us to our room, which, of course, was my old bedroom. The blue walls were still there, along with my old work desk, though all my posters had been taken down. The bed had been replaced, along with the closet. Grinning at us from the bed was the big stuffed Elmo I had as a kid. Jadyn raced to the toy and gave it a big sniff.

"Mmmm. I love these old smells," she said. Then she looked at me in surprise. "Babe? You okay?"

"Yeah," I said, grabbing Elmo from her and giving it a hug.

"I'm so glad you're home again," Jadyn said, smiling as she began to undress.

I whistled and gave her a quick spank on the butt. "I'm glad you got to come along."

As Jadyn disappeared to the bathroom to take a shower, I flopped onto the bed. Apart from Aunt Beth's news about Shannon, I was actually feeling okay. This trip wasn't even about me. It was about my aunt, and I had to focus on her. They would get married in less than a week, and I was happy I was going to be there to cheer them on. Jadyn and I would be flying home

196

before we knew it.

Yes. It was all going to be okay.

CHAPTER 3

AUNT BETH AND RICKY GOT MARRIED in the lush backyard of a folksy lakeside resort. I'd never seen her look so happy, and Ricky was looking every bit the proud man now that he was her husband—and almost completely unrecognizable in his tailor-made suit. The weather was good: it was pleasantly hot, the sky was brighter than bright for once, and light winds made sure we weren't actually sweating.

Jadyn kept commenting how hot I looked in a suit. She had a thing for me in suits. She was wearing a light blue sundress with bows on top of her shoulders, and the dress swished about royally in the breeze. The heels she had on made her almost as tall as I was. She was stunning.

During the afterparty, Jadyn and I drifted toward the dance floor. Aunt Beth had invited way more people than I'd expected, and the backyard was becoming just a little congested.

"I can't wait for our big day…" Jadyn whispered in my ear as we danced.

I grinned. "I don't think you'll have to wait all that long," I whispered back.

Jadyn bit her lip and looked at me with awe in her eyes. I knew exactly what she was imagining.

The sun rapidly began to fade into the horizon, the winds picking up and the sky darkening into a dreamy orange-purple sunset. As soon as we took a break, some cheery-looking kid guy walked up to Jadyn and handed her a rose, politely asking her to dance. Jadyn giggled and took off her strappy heels, handing them to me. I helped tuck the rose into one of the clips in her hair. I winked at the kid, and, not wanting to be the third wheel, headed to the bar and got myself a rum and Coke. I was happy to do some quiet, uninterrupted people watching, and thankfully there weren't a lot of people I recognized. The opposite was true too—a lot of the guests simply had no idea who I was, which I took as a compliment.

That was when I spotted her.

Her.

A shiver ran over me as I took her in. She was wearing a sleeveless yellow dress that looked a bit tight at the top and displayed her generously thick cleavage. She was dancing near a small crowd, her head swaying lightly to the beat, her hips shimmying in perfect rhythm. Her long, wavy blonde hair seemed uncurled from a previous updo, framing down her back with golden highlights. Her face was a little flushed from dancing. She looked so different, and yet she was the same old Shannon.

My stomach lurched as she dropped down to her heels and threw an arm in the air as she felt the music. I couldn't believe Aunt Beth had invited her. How could she? Why didn't she tell me?

Of course. Aunt Beth was just being nice. Everyone my age had left this stupid town, except for her. She'd assumed I wanted to meet her. Or that she wanted to meet me.

In that instant, she made eye contact. Her blue eyes shimmered underneath the fairy lights.

I froze.

In the few seconds it took for Shannon to walk over to me, I considered many things. Make a run for it. Scream until my lungs broke. Vomit into the grass. Throw my drink down her dress.

None of which, of course, I had time to do. Or the balls.

"Hey," Shannon said. Her tone was completely cool. Casual. "If it isn't Todd Coleman."

My head bristled as I processed the way she said my name. It had slipped out so easily, like it had been primed over the years, waiting for this exact moment. "If it isn't Shannon Kelley," I countered, but I wanted to fucking kick myself. *Fake. Fake. You're fake. So fucking fake.*

"You remember me," Shannon said, smiling. "So were you actually going to say hi? Or just watch me dance the whole night?"

Ugh. "I was…trying to place you."

A dig. She felt it. She looked down at the pair of heels I was clutching, then back at me. Had she seen me and my girlfriend together? I was willing to bet she had. Anger shot through me in the awkward silence that ensued. I hated her nonchalance, coming up to talk like she didn't have a clue she was the reason I'd had such shit self-esteem my whole life. The reason I couldn't even talk to a girl unless I was drunk. I wanted to be the bigger person, but all the memories were flooding back to me. The smell of the lockers. The bitter scent of smoke in that bathroom. Her body leaning over me, handing me her panties, telling me she needed me to wear them.

I had to say something. I couldn't let her brush something like this under the carpet like I was dog shit. I couldn't do that to myself. I wouldn't let her.

But as soon as I opened my mouth, Shannon was walking away, her butt swaying almost hypnotically.

No!

But all she did was walk to the side of the bar and wave me over. Like a robot, I followed her. All I could hear was my own heart beating wildly. It was like every sound—the laughter, the chatter, even the music—had vanished into the ether.

Shannon was looking at a polaroid camera set up with a big corkboard. The corkboard was decorated with pictures of wedding guests and had messages written on top of them.

"Want to wish your aunt together?" she asked.

"Uh," I said, my throat suddenly going dry.

Before I even said anything, Shannon had pulled me to her side. She took Jadyn's heels away from me and placed them gingerly on the grass. Her fingers grazed the side of my hand, instantly sending tingles prickling through my body. She smelled...sexy. She *was* sexy. There was no denying that truth. She pressed against me and I didn't dare breathe as I forced a smile for the camera. We waited in silence until it developed. I was looking every bit as pained as I felt in the photo, but Shannon didn't seem to notice.

She pinned the photo onto the wall and scribbled something against it, then handed the pen to me.

"Are you staying here for long?" she asked.

"No," I said curtly, writing down all the nonsensical words that came to my head. "We're leaving tomorrow."

"Oh," she said. *Was she disappointed?* "Such a short visit. That's too bad."

"Too bad?" My voice was coming back to me, and along with it, my balls. "Why?"

She flicked her eyes at me. "I'm sure your aunt would've liked you to stay longer." The judgemental look was souring her face. "I was honestly surprised you even came for the wedding. It was like you forgot she even existed. She was really hurt, you know."

Hurt? Who the fuck was Shannon, telling people about being hurt?

"I think you know as well as I do why I stayed away," I said in a small voice.

"Hmm," Shannon said, then let out a scathing laugh. This was it. This was the Shannon I remembered. That same laugh. She was still the same. She was refusing to admit anything. "Where are you staying?"

"Aunt Beth's place," I said, then reflexively asked: "You?"

"The same old house," she said. "Michael moved in right after we got married, and then we renovated the whole place. Mom and Dad moved out because they were done with this town. Funny, I know."

I knew the route to that house like the back of my hand. I wondered where her husband was.

Shannon knew exactly what I was thinking.

"Michael couldn't be here because he had a gig booked like a year back." Shannon was watching me closely as she explained.

"Out of town. I'm home all day tomorrow, if you want to come over."

What? I blinked at her, sure that I'd misheard things. Did she just invite me to her place? While her husband was still out of town?

"I can't," I finally said. "I'm taking Jadyn out tomorrow. We don't really have much time, since we have an early morning flight the day after, so…" This time, I was the one watching her closely, looking to see her reaction. "Jadyn's my girlfriend."

Shannon just nodded. "She's pretty," she said absent-mindedly. Her finger was tracing over the guest messages on the wall. I hated that a picture of Shannon and I was immortalized on there. "I never thought you had it in you to pull a girl like that, Todd."

I grimaced. The insult had cut through me hard, razor sharp and biting. I was old Todd then, the skinny guy with long hair and acne, the guy who she turned into a girl.

Shannon sighed. "In case you change your mind…" she said. "You know what to do."

"Okay."

And just like that, she left. Right after she'd insulted me. Right after knocking any shred of normality left in my world. She stepped through the crowds, and walked back up the steps through the resort doors, disappearing from view.

"Who was that?"

Jadyn came through, hooking her arm through mine. She was red-faced from dancing, and the rose in her hair was no longer there, probably fallen and crushed on the dance floor.

"Just an old friend," I choked out.

"Oh," she said, completely disinterested. "Well, I'm famished. Let's go eat."

I let her pull me away to the buffet, but I was far from hungry.

CHAPTER 4

THE NEXT DAY, JADYN AND I HAD the house to ourselves. Aunt Beth and Ricky had flown to Cancun for their honeymoon, but we were basically given the house key so we could make ourselves at home during our final day in town. Our flight was at an ungodly hour the next day (4 a.m.), and with our late start to the morning, we didn't really have much time. Jadyn did some shopping on the little strip of indie shops downtown and we chilled at the pool hall. Then I took her out for dinner. We had wine and pasta in one of the more upscale restaurants that Aunt Beth had recommended.

The whole time I was with Jadyn, I was trying to push Shannon's invitation out of my head.

A part of me still couldn't believe I'd actually met her last night. That she'd actually asked me to *come over*. For what? Did she want to apologize to me? Make amends? Somehow I doubted that. I remembered the way she'd danced so seductively under the lights, knowing that I'd been secretly watching her. The way she'd smelled and pulled me close for the picture. Ten years on, what the hell did she want to do to me? What more could she take from me?

Once we came home, Jadyn announced she was exhausted. I wondered what Shannon was up to right then. Was she home alone? Probably looking after her kid?

Was she thinking about me?

Jadyn was huddled in bed. She was watching me pace up and down the room.

"Come here," she said.

I went over and climbed under the comforter. We snuggled.

"Are you okay?" she asked.

I nodded. "Just a little tired. I guess."

"This doesn't have to be your last day, Todd," Jadyn said. "We can come again. Soon. Maybe even next summer. I know how important Aunt Beth is to you."

I nodded again. "Yeah, that would be nice," I lied. I gave her a peck on the cheek.

"I'll be going to bed soon."

"Okay," I said. I got out of bed and stretched. "I think I'll go get some fresh air. Maybe take a walk."

"Right now?"

"Yeah. Is that okay?"

"Of course it is." Jadyn smiled and took her phone, opening up her TikTok app. "Enjoy your walk. Time for some mindless scrolling before bed."

I left her there, slipping out the front door and locking it behind me. Outside, the air smelled sweet and earthy, and the starless sky seemed to stretch for miles beyond the darkness of the streets. I started walking, not thinking, trying not to untangle what I was really about to do. This was my last day. When would I come by again? Probably never. I had a very small window of opportunity. The question was: what the hell should I do?

My mind had already been made up. That was what scared me.

I just need closure, I thought as I upped my pace to a brisk walk. *I just need her to know what she made me feel.*

Shannon lived about twenty minutes away, right next to the community park. I knew the route by heart because I'd passed that way so many times all those years ago. I started a light jog, feeling my underarms dampen and my muscles loosen as I moved swiftly through the darkness. Jadyn was probably asleep by now. Maybe Shannon was too. A sense of dread settled over me as I walked past the familiar convenience store and made a left onto Shannon's street. I was being stupid. Shannon was never going to answer the fucking door.

I passed through each house, trying to catch my breath. I could see the park in the distance, shrouded in misty shadows. And then there it was. Shannon's old place.

I walked up to the front door. The lights were on both upstairs and downstairs, and there was the faint buzz of a television, but other than that, it was quiet. Way too quiet. The quietness was strangely inviting.

No husband. No one home except for my bully.

I don't have any bad intentions, I reminded myself.

I knocked on Shannon's door, and waited for her to answer.

CHAPTER 5

HER SON WAS SLEEPING in her arms.

If Shannon was surprised that I was standing on her front doorstep, she didn't show it. There wasn't a lick of makeup on her face, but her skin was flawless except for a slight puffiness under her eyes. She was wearing jeans and a rumpled T-shirt which exposed her belly button, giving away how tall she was. Her son was older than I'd expected—about four or five years old—and completely silent and content in the cocoon of his mother's warmth.

Shannon didn't close the door on me.

I followed her as she went to an upstairs bedroom and lay her son down, then stepped out and closed the door behind her.

"I was just about to take a shower," she said.

I swallowed. "Maybe I should go."

To my surprise she took my hand and held it there. "Don't leave," she said. "I didn't think you'd come." She led me to the living room sofa and motioned for me to sit down.

"I think we need to talk," she said, taking some of the

magazines off the sofa to make space for me. As I flopped down, her arm brushed against mine, lingering there for longer than it needed to be. The pit of my stomach began to flutter and my heart amped up so rapidly I felt it thunder inside my chest.

Shannon gave me a sideways glance. One corner of her mouth lifted up, the sweetness of temptation already playing on her lips. Those soft pink lips, devilishly reminding me of lips that belonged to another part of her.

"Just give me five minutes to rinse myself off. I trust you'll be quiet?" she said, nudging her head toward the upstairs bedroom.

I struggled to speak. "Of course."

She gave me a nod and disappeared out of the room. I patted the phone inside my pocket, wondering if I should send Jadyn a quick message to say I dropped by a friend's house. But then I decided against it—Jadyn was sleeping, after all, and I didn't want to bother her. And what the fuck was I thinking would happen tonight? I was already reading too much into things, when Shannon had explicitly stated that all she'd wanted to do was *talk*.

I stared at the TV, the images just all blurring together into a mess. My chest felt unspeakably tight and I couldn't feel my feet on the floor. Some time later, Shannon came back into the room. Her hair was wet, the ends trailing down her shoulders all the way to her hips.

She was dressed in just a towel.

I suddenly couldn't breathe. Every thought and all sense of logic escaped me.

Shannon stepped up to me and straddled me, her body arching until her ass settled down confidently on my lap. Her wet hair swept against my T-shirt, sending droplets of shower water flying onto me. She gave me a criminally beautiful smile.

"What are you— " I choked.

"Shhh. Undress me," she said, taking my hand and guiding me to the small towel knot near her armpit.

My fingers were shaking as I undid her towel and it fell off in a crumpled heap by my feet. Her huge breasts sprung into my face, causing my cock to twitch uncontrollably. Her entire weight was on my cock, and it felt magical.

My bully took my hand and guided it toward one of her breasts. I gave it a squeeze and bit back a moan. Her nipples were so red and puffy and as hard as bullets. She whipped them in my face, dragging one nipple up and down my mouth. The room was becoming hazy, and so were my thoughts.

"I have a girlfriend!" I finally sputtered out. "This is wrong. I shouldn't be…"

But Shannon just put a finger to my lips. "I know you want this, Todd. You've wanted this for years, haven't you?"

She was so right I wanted to roll up into a ball and pass out.

I didn't want to face the truth. That I'd worshiped her. Even when she clearly hated me with every fiber of her being, I'd worshiped her. Dreamt of her. Wanted her. Loved her. Nothing—*nothing*—had changed in ten years.

"You broke me," I said, and suddenly I was blinking tears away. I was so frustrated at Shannon and angry at myself for not being able to hold my emotions together. "You broke me, Shannon. How could you do something like that to another person?"

Shannon was silent. Then she said, "Take off your shirt."

I didn't resist. Once my T-shirt was on the floor, Shannon

unbuckled my pants and slipped my boxers down to my knees. She stared at my hard-on like she was studying it from every angle. I was shaved. I made it a point to shave my cock and ass every day. It was something that Jadyn appreciated. Now, with one of the most intimate parts of me exposed, I had the feeling that Shannon wanted to touch it, maybe check how soft and smooth the skin was. And I did want her to touch it. So bad. I wanted to her grip it in her palm, kiss it, lick it, suck it, make love to it...

But she didn't touch me.

She got off the couch. Like she'd suddenly come to her senses. She took the towel off the floor and tied it around herself again, not even looking at me.

I suddenly felt very ashamed. What had I done? I'd been a fucking idiot. I'd never even thought about Jadyn. I'd already hurt the person I loved the most. I couldn't believe it.

Shannon breezed to the front door and unlocked it.

"If you want this, Todd, I'll be upstairs," she said quietly. "But you'll have to strip everything off before you come see me. And if you don't want to do this, you can walk out. I don't need to see you." She smiled brightly, her teeth unbelievably, perfectly white. "As for your girlfriend, I don't know her. I don't really give a fuck about her Todd. She's your problem."

I opened my mouth to speak, but she just ignored me and calmly walked out and back upstairs.

She was still so cruel. So, so cruel.

I had a million questions. What did she mean by *this*? Did she really mean sex? Would she really let me fuck her? Or was this a trap? Just another one of her plans to humiliate me?

With my erection slowly fading away, I considered my predicament. The answer was simple. I had to get the fuck out of here, back to Aunt Beth's house and back to my girlfriend, wash every dirty thought off me and then go to sleep. But I struggled to move to the front door, out onto the steps and into the night. This was like a fantasy. Shannon—the girl who had plagued me for years—wanted me.

And I needed her.

Needed her to touch me. Take control of me. Fill me with shame, and so much more.

Just like before.

As I stepped out of my boxers, becoming fully naked in a strange house, I knew I would never forgive myself. I'd failed myself, and I'd failed Jadyn. My renewed boner completely defied my conscience as I slowly made my way up the staircase. I could hear the faint sounds of the washer running behind a closed door. At the end of the hallway I found myself in Shannon's bedroom.

Shannon and *Michael's* bedroom.

She was in bed, in a worn pink robe, reading an old paperback. When she heard me enter she took off her glasses and set the book aside. She glanced at my naked body, at my erection, but didn't say anything. Her robe parted a little, revealing the curves of her cleavage. My breath hitched as a swollen nipple popped out into the open.

My gaze fell to the spread of clothes on top of the bedspread. It was a white, angelic looking lingerie set. Satin panties. A bra with petite ribbons coming down the straps. White stockings with a floral design at the top. A garter belt that had cut-outs in the shape of hearts.

We didn't exchange a single word.
I knew what I had to do.

CHAPTER 6

I CREPT FORWARD, MY PENIS BOBBING with every step.

I suddenly felt ashamed of my boner, too shy to appear masculine.

That was how she wanted me after all. Small, delicate, devoted and feminine. A victim.

I picked up the women's undergarments and balled them up against my crotch. Slouching, I made my way toward the bathroom. But then Shannon finally spoke, her words slicing through the unbelievably thick tension in the air.

"Where do you think you're going?" she said. "You can dress up right here."

I cringed. Humiliated, I turned around. Yes, this was just dress up after all. I was becoming a woman to entertain her.

As she watched me get dressed, I knew that she knew. From the way the panties slinked up my body, settling gracefully on my hips, to the way I hooked up the bra so easily behind my back, adjusting the straps and cups so they fit my chest better. She was the only person in the world who knew my secret. I brought the garter belt up to my waist, not being able to help but admire the way it shaped my body so beautifully. I hooked it close and fell down on the bed next to her, feeling her shallow breaths ghost over my back as the white stockings glided over my legs. I stood up and clipped the garter belt onto the stockings, adjusting the strap length.

Shannon smiled once I was done. Then she got off the bed and headed straight to the closet, taking out a tube of lipstick and a long golden-brown wig. She sauntered over to me and asked me to kneel in front of her. She uncapped the lipstick and hovered it over my mouth. I pouted like a good girl, rubbing my lips together once she'd finished applying the deep orange-red color onto me. I desperately wanted to please her.

She warmed a little lipstick in between her fingers and dabbed some onto my cheeks and eyelids. Her touch made me want to groan out loud.

"I bet your girlfriend doesn't do this," she said as she slid the wig over my head and fixed it.

The words shot through me like an arrow. It was unforgivable, but there was something about the way she said that that made me *so* horny. Shannon was so fucking seductive. She knew the power she had, and she was brandishing it over me like a warrior woman with a sword. My boner grew underneath my soft, satin panties. Soon, I knew I'd be leaking.

I was still kneeling on the carpet when she hunched over, laying her weight atop my shoulders and straddling my face. I brought my arms up around her thighs and took in my bully's scent. The need within me was so primal now, and nothing could stop me from waltzing straight into this disaster.

Shannon started to gyrate against my face, swiped her pussy slowly up and down, using my nose as a spur.

"Do I smell better than your girlfriend?" she asked huskily.

I tensed, feeling faint and weakened at the question. How could I even answer that? I couldn't do that to Jadyn.

"Answer me, you piece of shit," Shannon said, pushing my head back so I would look at her.

I recoiled physically at that insult. I stared deep into the shimmering blue pools of her eyes, savoring the attention she was giving me.

"And you better not call me anything but Goddess," she said, parting her thighs so I could speak. "Because that's what I am to you. So answer me, Todd. Fucking answer me. Don't be a coward, like you were in school. Be brave. Be who you are."

"You smell better than my girlfriend, Goddess," I said, my voice tinny and girly.

She nudged my chin upwards, forcing me to look up at her again. "Say her name."

I took a deep breath. "You...you smell better than Jadyn, Goddess," I said. *Fuck*. I'd done it. I'd betrayed my girlfriend in the most heinous way possible.

My hurt seemed to fuel Shannon's arousal. She started pumping up and down, stimulating herself freely on my lipsticked mouth. "Lick me, sissy," she said, her voice rasping in the quiet, still room.

I did it obediently, slowly, until I was engulfed in her juices. She was so wet. She cried and groaned desperately, her thighs shivering with pleasure as her clit danced against my tongue. I was surrounded by her from every possible angle, and I loved it.

I inserted my fingers inside her, sucking at her hot, hard clit like I was in a rage.

"I wonder how Jadyn would feel if she knew you were out here, licking me like a dog," she moaned. "Dressed in panties and a bra with makeup and a wig on. Like a little slut. What do you think she'd do, sissy?"

Before I could react, however, her body slipped into an amazing climax. She squeezed her legs together and humped me violently, sputtering out moans that were half-silenced only by her need to be quiet, her nails almost skinning my bare shoulders. A minute later, she finally pulled away, letting me breathe.

"Jadyn will never forgive me, Goddess," I whispered, feeling my privates thump painfully underneath my panties. "Why are you doing this to me, Goddess? Why do you hate me so much?"

Shannon stood up and gave me a disgusted look. Her thighs were still glistening with her fluids. "Me? I'm not doing anything," she lashed out. "You're the one who came here. You're the one who came upstairs to our room. You did this to yourself, sissy."

My chin trembled. I wasn't willing to let her go so easily this time. "I mean, back in school," I said quietly. "I want to know why you bullied me. You had such…hate…for me." I bit my lip, fighting against the urge to sob in front of her. "That day in the bathroom? It really fucked me up, you know. More than you'd ever know."

Shannon wrapped her robe around her and fished something out from a bag under the bed before opening up the door to the bedroom balcony. I followed her, reluctant at first to step out into a more public space wearing what really was a very sexy lingerie set. But Shannon ordered me to close the balcony door behind us and then lit up her cigarette, glancing just once at my disdainful expression.

"Don't look at me like that, sissy. I quit," she said, taking a long drag and exhaling into the night air. "This is the first I've had in like three years." She swiveled toward me, resting her back against the wall. I couldn't help but blush, resting my arms over my crotch. She was still looking at me with so much hunger. "I mean, look at you. Why did I torment you? The answer is simple, simpler than you think. I liked you."

"I don't believe you," I blurted out.

This time, she blew smoke straight into my face, causing me to fumble back while she let out an amused giggle. "Maybe liked is the wrong word...maybe I liked the fact I could treat you like shit and you still respected me. You were falling head over heels for me, and I guess I liked the way you made me feel. I'm not saying what I was doing was healthy. It was an addiction." She laughed. "Look at me, doing so much *self-reflecting.*"

"Are you happy, Shannon?" I asked. "I mean, Goddess? In your marriage?"

She answered instantly. "Of course I am. Michael's fucking great. I have a family now, and I love them to death." She gave me a hard stare, and this time goosebumps cropped up all over my arms. "I can tell you love Jadyn to death too. But sex is different, huh?"

An icy chill twisted down my spine. I wanted to call her out so badly. Shannon was probably fucking someone behind her husband's back every time she got the chance, and tonight was really just one of her average adventures. But really—was I any different? Cheat once, cheat twice, it was all the same. I was just as bad as her.

Shannon tossed the cigarette onto the balcony floor and stomped on it once. "Anyway, enough talking. The Goddess is ready."

"What is Goddess ready for?" I asked meekly, feeling something spark inside my very core.

"She's ready to fuck you," Shannon said.

She snorted at my incredulous face. "Don't tell me you didn't think that was in the cards for tonight?" Her eyes trailed from my head to my breasts, to my waist cinched in tight by the garter belt, to my legs, bathed in white. "Yes, I want to fuck you, sissy girl, and you know exactly what that means, don't you? You're smart enough to know that. Ugh, when you're looking all sexy like that, I don't think I could forgive myself if I let you go tonight and *don't* fuck you. I mean, who knows when we'll see each other again?" We ambled back to the bedroom. "Come up here on the bed. No. On second thought, get down here. I like the thought of fucking you on the floor."

She pointed to the corner of the room that met with the bedroom door.

"Bend over and lean your shoulders against the door. Better be quick, sissy. We both don't have much time."

Nervously, I glanced at the clock. One hour to midnight. In less than five hours I'd be hopping on a plane, leaving my hometown forever. I prayed that Jadyn was fast asleep by now. I'd left my phone downstairs and now there was no way to know if she'd sent me any texts.

As I crawled into position, resting my right shoulder gently against the door, I felt so fucking small, so vulnerable, knowing what my bully was about to do to me. Shannon gave me a cryptic smile before ordering me to look straight at the door. Then I felt her foot skating up and down my back. I held my breath as she pulled on the panties, bringing them down little by little until my ass was fully exposed. She snuck a toe in between my cheeks, moving it so slowly, teasing me with her vulgar intentions.

When her toe tucked itself into the entrance of my asshole, I choked back a moan.

"Have you ever had sex with a man?"

"No, Goddess," I whispered. Then I made it a point to say: "I'm not gay, Goddess."

"I already know your girlfriend doesn't peg you," she said with a satisfied chuckle. "So. I'll assume you're a virgin."

"Nothing's been up there, other than some of my fingers, Goddess," I answered truthfully.

"Okay," she said. She was drizzling lube all over my crack. "Then hurry up and prep yourself. Use your fingers."

I whimpered. There was a hurried intensity to the way she was talking to me and it was turning me on so much—like she wanted to use me just to get her fix and then be done with me. Like I was just an itch she wanted to scratch. I smeared the lube all over my backside, feeling my privates squeeze out a ton of precum. Hastily, I inserted a finger inside my hole, finding the wetness of the lube a little too pleasurable.

As I made myself ready, Shannon was attaching a strap-on onto herself. The thing had two prongs sticking out, a big one from the front and a smaller one from the back. She inserted the smaller prong into her pussy and waved her new cock in my face.

The cock was a shiny peach, with a thick, fleshy head and light blue veins criss-crossing down the shaft.

Suddenly, I wanted to humiliate myself by telling her how much I really wanted her.

"Oh Goddess, I really need your cock inside me!" I cried out.

She flashed me a satisfied smirk.

"You're going to make me feel so good..." she said softly. "You think your ass knows how lucky it is tonight?"

I groaned. My finger was still inside my hole, vigorously rubbing in the lube.

Shannon came and stood over me. Her nakedness was dizzyingly beautiful. Her big breasts were swollen with arousal, and that pink cock seemed like it was every bit a part of her.

"Suck me," she said, getting down to her knees.

I sucked her eagerly, desperately, wanting to do more to please her, wishing I could do more to impress her. With every passing second, I hated my performance more and more, and tried to make up for it by being aggressive. I spat on her cock's mushroom head, then sloshed my mouth in and out, pumping the shaft with one frenzied palm. I could hear the other end of the dildo ram in and out of her increasingly wet pussy. The sound was like music to my ears.

"Look at you...sucking my big cock..." Shannon murmured. "Still a sissy and a loser, aren't you?"

I moaned into her cock, nodding frantically, accepting the bitter truth. I kept sucking until I could see her eyes cloud over with a lustful rage and she ordered me to stop.

"I'm going to fuck you now," she whispered, pushing my panties down further. She didn't have to state the obvious, but for some reason, the words reverberated in the air and soaked deep into my bones, making me shiver. I was overwhelmed—with excitement, with fear, with nerves. After all these years, my bully was going to fuck me.

I'd waited so long for this moment.

CHAPTER 7

WHEN SHANNON'S HUGE COCK FINALLY pierced me, it was like a decade of pain and frustration erupted out of me, causing me to shake and writhe against the door.

She was slow and gentle only for a short while. We didn't have a ton of time, after all, and her impatience was quickly taking over. I curled forward as she fucked me, my kneecaps digging painfully onto the floor, feeling her cock fill me and the pressure shoot up my tight virgin asshole. I'd made a mess of the carpet because I was steadily dripping onto it.

I tried not to think about anything other than this moment. Tried not to think of anyone other than my Goddess. I didn't want to face the future or worry about what would happen once all this was over.

And as my body gave in to my sinful urges and loosened itself, I bounced my butt to help her ram her penis even deeper into my depths.

It was all starting to feel unbearably, *dangerously* good.

"Break me, Goddess," I begged. "Break me so I won't even

be able to walk tomorrow. Break me so Jadyn will notice and have to ask me what's wrong. Break me so I'll have no choice but to tell her the truth. About what a pathetic sissy I am. A sissy who likes wearing panties and worshiping women who just want to use me."

I heard Shannon suck in a breath and then her cock twisted and jerked sharply into me. I bit down on my scream.

"Get over here," she rasped, throwing me against the foot of the bed. I was slumped over the edge, still on my knees, thighs spread wide for her. Shannon slithered her cock up and down my crack and the bottom of my back, teasing me until I didn't know whether I was whimpering or sobbing. Then she lined her soft legs against mine and started fucking my brains out again. My entire body bobbed with her thrusts, my head being jerked wildly in response to her fury. She fucked me again and again and again until I was just crying *oh god...oh god...oh god...*straight into the mattress.

And I couldn't help but think about Jadyn. My sweet, sweet Jadyn. She was back home, still sleeping, completely oblivious to what her sissy boyfriend was up to...

"Do you think Jadyn has cheated on me, Goddess?" I whimpered.

"If she hasn't already, she will," Shannon said. "It's only a matter of time, baby. You won't be able to keep up the pretense for much longer...she'll need to go looking for man dick...even *my* dick is much bigger and better than your crummy clit, isn't that right, baby?"

"Yes, Goddess!" I gasped.

She grabbed me roughly by the hips as she tanked into me with fresh energy. I pulled my long hair to the front and twisted sideways, wanting her to see my small breasts bounce each time she drilled me. My ass felt so sore already.

"Don't you fucking dare cum," she said, slapping me hard on one cheek.

Tears sprung down my rosy cheeks at her command. I was so close. *God, I need this. I need this. I need this.* I wasn't sure if I could control myself for much longer.

"Up," Shannon said suddenly.

The dildo slipped out of my ass, leaving my hole puckering and needy. She hoisted me up, pulling me painfully by one bra strap out of the bedroom.

"Stay quiet," she said.

"Yes, Goddess," I whispered.

I could hear the blood pounding in my head as I limped behind her. My legs were practically jelly.

Where was Shannon taking me?

CHAPTER 8

THE HOUSE ITSELF WAS SILENT APART FROM the patter of rain outside and the sweeping of tree branches against the windows. Winds howled over the roof like ghosts shrieking in disapproval at what we were doing. The only lights were coming from the living room downstairs. Shannon took me to the staircase and after going down halfway, she sat down on one of the stairs and parted her legs wide open, resting her elbows comfortably behind her. Her cock jerked up majestically, somehow looking bigger and more menacing. *Was that thing really inside me just a second ago?*

"Ride me," she ordered.

The butterflies in my stomach went crazy. *So hot. Soooo hot.* Holding onto the railing, I steadily lowered myself onto her. As her cock filled me again and I was brave enough to wrap my arms around her neck, I felt small again, tiny and worthless next to her tall, sinewy frame. I began to ride her, first testing it slowly to make sure my ass was up for it, then upping my pace, until I had no choice but to hand all my power to her.

"Oh fuck!" she gasped, falling back and letting go of me for a split second.

I must be making her feel good.

"I think...I think..."" I huffed, trying so hard but unable to form a coherent sentence. I was trying to tell her I was going to explode soon, and there was nothing I could do to stop it.

Using her teeth, Shannon pushed down one of my bra cups and attacked my nipple angrily with her tongue. Her left hand shot up to clamp over my mouth so I couldn't cry out in ecstasy. Her tongue twirled lustfully over my bud and then she was kissing it with furious desperation.

That was when I remembered the front door was still unlocked. My clothes were just feet away, along with my phone, and I could've sworn I was hearing it buzz. As I strained my ears, though, the buzzing faded away, and I knew it was just my imagination. But the thought of Shannon's husband cutting his trip short and waltzing in right through that door made me...wet. Our terrible secret uncovered...all he'd see would be my hot sissy ass bouncing on top of his wife's giant strap-on...

"Fuck me harder, Goddess!" I breathed.

"I'll fuck you, you whore," she whispered, letting a trail of saliva break as she released my abused nipple. Her fingers were suddenly on my sissy clit, which was brushing up against her belly and ruining it with precum. "Tell me the truth, whore. Tell me you love me."

"I love you, Goddess," I cried out, her fast pumping making me let go. "I love you! I love you! I love you!"

We came together that night. Shannon jerked around in her climax, ramming into me harder than she ever had, and I could almost feel the force of her pussy reverberating in my ass. My cum spraying onto her open hand was probably the most beautiful thing I'd ever seen. My groin twitched and squeezed upon itself like it was having a fucking seizure, the rush still just as intense as when it had started. I'd never had an orgasm even close to this in my life.

Once we were done, Shannon smeared my cum over my made-up face while I groaned in delight.

Then she stood up, unbuckled her strap-on, and just looked at me for a long time, as if memorizing everything she did to me so she could look back on this for years to come. I stared back at her, sitting on the step with my hair all wild and messy, sweat and cum running down my face, one nipple out, one expensive stocking torn to shreds.

"You can leave now," she said.

My mouth fell open. She was done with me. As soon as she'd cum, she wanted me out?

Had anything changed? Did this encounter even mean anything?

Wordlessly, I got up and walked to the living room. She followed me there and watched me strip down again. I gathered up her clothes and handed them to her along with the wig, giving her a sheepish smile.

I got dressed quickly, and when I turned around once more I thought I saw a single tear roll down her cheek.

I wanted to hug her so badly, but I didn't want her to lash out at me.

Don't be a coward.

"Fuck it," I muttered. I went in and wrapped my arms around

her, surrounding myself in her scent. Then I gave her a kiss on the cheek.

To my surprise, she hugged me back.

"Sorry for ruining your underwear," I whispered.

All she did was smile back.

"Get out," she said. The smile actually reached her eyes this time.

I began walking back in the rain, letting my face and clothes soak in the downpour. I was definitely having trouble walking straight and every limb in my body felt battered with fatigue. Thoughts of Jadyn ripped through me, and I was suddenly nauseous. I pulled out my phone and peered down at the screen. No calls or messages.

I'd have to break it to her—I knew that much. She deserved to know. An image of her all bundled up in bed like a sleeping koala—that was how she slept—tugged at my heart. Maybe the time wasn't now, but it would have to happen soon.

I started jogging, desperate to go back to Aunt Beth's house, back to my girlfriend, and back to my old life as quickly as I could.

THE END

Thank you for reading!
Lots of love,
Rae

ABOUT THE AUTHOR

A full-time content writer by day and an erotica writer by night, Rae Robinson writes all kinds of dirty stories when the doors are locked and anything can happen. Her main interests include femdom, sissification, and feminization. She particularly loves exploring the intersection between sexuality and self-identity.

Printed in Great Britain
by Amazon

37665657R00136